# Back To Now

## CATHLEEN ELLIS

Cover design by Launie Parry
Interior design by Brian Schwartz

ISBN: 978-1629672311
Library of Congress Control Number: 2022901274

# YOUNG PEOPLE IN LOVE
## IN THE HEARTLAND OF AMERICA

# OTHER BOOKS BY CATHLEEN ELLIS
### www.CathleenEllis.com

# 1

**"Blessed beyond measure to have my life" - Kate**

Friday, December 15, 2006, Porttown, Iowa

"You're just awesome as Gabriella," Emma Chavez turned as she spoke to Kate Reynels in the back seat. Pete Duncan drove, and he echoed Emma's compliment.

"I'm so glad we got to see the performance tonight. I think we're one of the first high schools in the whole country to perform *High School Musical*."

"Hey, that might be right, Pete. And Emma, I appreciate your compliment, makes me feel fuzzy warm, done good. Mom and dad'll see me perform tomorrow night. After we'll strike the set, and yum, yum, celebrate with pizza and pop up on the stage."

"You guys, maybe, will perform a scene or two."

"Yeah, Pete, we may decide to do that to help remember the play. Hey and there's a book that's come out about the play. I want to see how the book works out the scenes, the dancing."

"Uh, where's Evan?"

"Ah, Evan," she whispered, "I totally love you." She patted her heart and paused, "Uh, he's with guy friends. We don't, well, can't spend much time together. I still babysit a lot, and he works in the downtown hardware store."

"Evan did a great job, opposite you, as Troy. He loves you, and you him, kinda like a love light shown all around you two."

"Yeah, he's so uber talented, dancing, singing, acting. Isn't much he can't accomplish. Guys, thanks for driving me home."

 howtosay

Kate arrived at the Miloh home at 7:30 the next morning. The three kids sat at the kitchen island eating their usual cereals and having toast, slathered with strawberry jelly, their favorite.

"You folks, wow, very nice," Kate smiled to the handsome couple, him dark haired and brown-eyed, and her a blue-eyed tall woman with wheat blonde hair.

"Yeah, Kate, we clean up pretty good, for stuff like weddings."

Kate laughed as the couple gave each other a peck on their cheeks and kissed their children goodbye. She checked the kitchen clock and noted the time.

"By noon I'll drive my car home, have the afternoon to get homework done and get ready for my final performance," she spoke out loud.

Sam Miloh looked at Kate, "Did you dance good last night, Katie?"

"I did, gonna show you three a little dance step I did."

She flew around the kitchen area performing a dance step and singing a short piece of a song.

Annie Miloh, four, shouted out, "Yay, Katie, you're so pretty when you dance and sing."

"Thank you, Annie. You know how to make me feel good."

"Katie nice."

Kate stood straight and tall next to Abby's high-chair and helped her finish up her oat cereal.

"Why thank you, Abby, you already give compliments. Hey, that sure makes me feel warm and happy. Oh, you all praise me," she said as she gazed at her three charges. She gave each of them a hug.

Once breakfast and clean up finished the four of them bundled up and went to the backyard to play. The kids had swings, a fort, a sandbox, and lots of trucks and toys for hauling stuff.

By mid-afternoon Kate finished her homework and lay down to rest, before having an early dinner. For days now she tingled from excitement, having the lead, Gabriella, in the play and having her special friend, Evan, as the male lead. And Christmas was coming.

"I love this time of the year; the Christ Child born, and folks in good moods. Our country, we're sure having good times right now, and God, I'm grateful, for all I have," she prayed out loud, "my family, home, the education I'm getting, and all the special training my folks've made sure I have."

She hugged her parents as she got ready to leave.

"We're excited to see you perform tonight, Kate. It'll be late, right, with striking the set?"

"Yeah, and food, thank you for your contribution for the food."

Kate remembered her parents giving her money for the pizza and pop after the final presentation.

&

"Group hug, cast, group hug," Mrs. Shalmer, the director, spoke out after the curtain closed and the cast and crew stood, lined up on the stage, holding hands. Applause still rang in their ears.

Kate looked around, seeing the students, some with happy tears, and others, with kind of shocked looks at the play finally being completed. In a few minutes the cast and crew began the preliminary steps to take down the tall and awkward sets they used for the play's background. They took a short break to enjoy the delicious pizza and sodas.

"Happy time, a job well done," is what the cast and helpers spoke, smiling to each other. "And it was a ton of work, but oh so rewarding."

Then the students got after it to finish up their work.

Kate moved near a set behind the curtains after it got placed along the wall, for movement to the storage area. Suddenly the set shuddered and began to fall after Kate accidently moved her leg into the set. The set fell forward, catching Kate's head, throwing her to the floor. She saw something dark, black.

The group heard the crash and the silence after. They ran toward the noise.

"Oh dear God, It's Kate."

"Stay back," a student hollered out.

Evan saw the blood on the stage floor under Kate's head as he knelt next to her. He placed his hand on her carotid artery and felt the pump, pump of her heart. The students gathered and in slow motion moved the set away from Kate's head and body.

"911's been called," a parent spoke out.

"We need to wait for the ambulance; they'll move her the way they want."

The director gave orders, and the stage began to be cleared. Many of the cast and crew cried.

Their director called them together, "Each in your own way, pray for Kate. She's unconscious; some of you saw the gash in the back of her head from the set's impact. And we don't know about the front of her skull. By tomorrow the doctors will know more. She'll be at Memorial."

"Mrs. Shalmer, maybe a CT scan, or an MRI?"

"Yes, that can help diagnose how her head is."

ॐ

1 a.m., Sunday, December 17, 2006, Porttown Memorial Hospital

David and Ann Reynels stood on either side of Kate, holding her hands.

"We're admitting her," the ER doctor gazed at Kate's parents. "We have the wound to her front forehead patched up; five butterfly bandages fixed it. We're hoping for no scarring."

"She musta landed face down," David turned to his wife.

"The gash to the back of her head, where the wooden board from the set hit her, that's deeper, and required seven stitches. We cut away a little section of her hair to fix it. But that's not our concern. She'll go to the neuro unit," the ER doctor paused, "they'll do a CT scan, for sure, to ascertain the extent of Kate's concussion. And an MRI, it might be necessary. Please go home and get some sleep. She may be unconscious for more time. I'd suggest you return tomorrow morning. We'll continue to give her fluids by IV. And the folks upstairs will take over."

℘

Thursday, December 12, 1946, Riverdawn, Iowa

"Go, Holly, I'll put Maggie down for her nap after I read her a story."

"I told her you would read her *The Little Engine That Could.* Thanks, Mom, for staying with her so I can work my Tuesday and Thursday afternoon shifts at the library. Please put the shepherd's pie in the oven at 5, 300 degrees; it'll take an hour, uh, everything's cooked, just needs warming up."

"Will do, thanks for preparing that. And this is my pleasure, it's my special twice a week time with my granddaughter."

"And I've my special time, the library, just a great place, and I get to visit with folks."

Holly gave her blonde daughter a hug, "Bye, sweet Maggie."

She hugged her mom.

"I love you, Mom."

She stood away from her mom and grabbed her hands and squeezed them. "And you know how much I appreciate you helping me."

After looking out the front window and seeing the many inches of snow on the front lawn, she decided to put on her heavy boots and walk to the library.

"I'm stretching my legs; it'll give me a chance to plan out the next two weeks in my head. Oh, Christmas is coming; the war's over. This year, like the end of last year, my prayer, and that of many people, is hope for a better world. And this afternoon, the sun warms me from the cold. Anyway I'm so blessed, to have Jake and Maggie, my folks and Jake's folks, and a nice home, that we're able to rent, thanks to Jake's great job," she whispered.

She ran up the steps and opened the heavy wooden door into the city library. She took in a deep breath, the pungent odor of aging books, and heard quiet. Kate decided that sometimes she swore she could hear the authors whispering to her, from their respective books. Her imagination took that over as she spent time reshelving the rows and rows of books .

"Holly, glad you're here. Jane went home sick, so there're lots of books to reshelve," Mary, the assistant librarian, smiled to her.

Holly set her purse under the counter and hung up her coat on the rack.

"Happy to be here; it's a small way I can serve my community, and to help out with family finances."

"That's right, dear girl," Mary gazed at Holly with her shining blonde hair and blue eyes. "Oh, and in the work room there are several new books; they are flagged and stacked up high, for us to put out special for the holidays."

Holly got to work, humming *White Christmas*. She heard it on the radio, the station she listened to all day long at home. Bing Crosby, a favorite singer of hers, sang the song. She wasn't sure about all the lyrics, so she kept humming.

She stepped into the workroom, still humming. She twirled around, did dance steps that took her to the shelf she needed. She remembered *Arsenic and Old Lace* and how excited she felt as a main character in that play her last year of high school.

"One of these days I want to teach dance, and acting. I had the training, but I'm not using it now. But pretty soon the country and our town will return to a kind of normal," she thought and nodded, as she stood on the top step of the two step ladder. It helped her reach the new books she needed to put out for the holidays.

With both hands she reached up and tried to pick up all the books. They seemed heavier than she expected. She set them back down and pulled just two of the books from the shelf. She turned to jump off the ladder with the books. To her horror and out of the corner of her eye she saw the shelf crashing down above her. She screamed and saw something dark, and then black.

Within a half hour the one ambulance in Riverdawn transported her to the town's hospital.

After two hours her husband, Jake Schoner, and her dad, Tom Deltan, came to be near her in the tiny Emergency area.

"Doc, how long do you think she'll be out?"

"Don't know, Jake, and Tom, from seeing war injuries, you know it could take time. I'll stitch up the cut on her forehead, probably three stitches, and we'll have to cut her blonde hair around the wound to the back of her head. I'm hoping she'll wake up before long. That's a big thing, how long they are unconscious. A concussion like this, it's hard to say, too much we still don't know about brain injuries."

"Maybe admit her overnight?"

"Let's see if she wakes up soon."

An hour later Holly still lay unconscious.

"Tom, I'll stay, go and have dinner with Ellie and Maggie."

Jake and his father-in law hugged and then he left. The technician took Holly to X-ray.

They returned as Jake paced the hall. The doctor came to Holly's bed.

"We need to admit Holly, hopefully just over the night. I looked at the X-ray and can't see anything abnormal. But, Jake," Dr. Abram shook his head, "remember that we're flying blind with a lot of stuff about the head. We're learning, from the blast injuries of soldiers during the war. But research, progress is slow. The gauge we use now, the longer Holly's unconscious, the more difficult her situation might be."

"Then," he paused and gazed at Holly, "I'll pray."

He prayed most of that night. Jake woke with a start, his head resting on Holly's bed in the ward where she got moved. It was 5 a.m. He stood up from the chair and looked down at her. He felt the pound pound of the ache at the top of his head, from resting on her bed, in that awkward position.

"She's so beautiful; that's a rough-looking lump on her forehead. Doc says she won't scar. And the wound on the back of her head, it'll heal, a couple stitches there. I love her so much. Holly's gotta get better; for our Maggie and for me," Jake spoke out as tears trickled down his face and onto the bed cover.

His mind sought images of his wife and daughter. Holly ran after Maggie as she toddled along in the backyard grass. Holly caught her blue-eyed, blonde daughter, picked her up and held her close as she danced around, circling and circling in the grass. His tears continued to dribble down his cheeks as he stepped away from her bed and out into the hall.

"God help us; it is up to You, after all," he mused after he paced in the hall. He used his handkerchief to mop up his face. Then he prayed, for her safe return to consciousness.

℘

Ellie took that Friday off from work at the library. She stayed with Maggie, and fixed breakfast for both of them. Tom called from the hospital at 7:30 a.m. Holly still lay unconscious. He cried, and Ellie cried, both at the same time over the phone. Holly never had anything serious happen to her before this time in her life.

Holly opened her eyes, seeing blurs at first. White shadows stood on both sides of her. She felt a light shine into each of her eyes.

"She's waking up," she heard a deep male voice in the background.

"God's blessing," she heard from another male voice.

She felt a kiss on her cheek.

"Welcome back, darling Holly, we been real worried," she heard a deep male voice say.

"My head hurts, so fierce. It's pounding, like a bass drum," she whispered.

She turned her head a little to the right and then a little to the left. She saw three people, one man on the side where she received the kiss on her cheek. And the other two were on the other side, one a man in a white coat, and another man who had one eye that continued to stare straight ahead at her.

"I'm sorry, but I don't know who you all are," she blurted out.

She turned her head from side to side and sobbed.

The doctor spoke to the two men outside the ward, "After a time unconscious, a patient may have some temporary amnesia. This is too much for her right now. It's good that you leave, go to work. Let us spend some time with Holly. We'll call Ellie with updates. If all goes well, we'll release her later today. Her headache probably will continue, for a time."

Jake and Tom nodded to the doctor and left for work. The doctor returned to Holly's bed with a young nurse.

"Holly, I'm Dr. Abram and this is Mrs. Lurner. She was a couple years ahead of you at Riverdawn High School. I'll let you two chat for a few minutes. She'll talk to you a bit, to help us assess you. Is that OK?"

"OK, they gave me a pill for my aching head; it's starting to work."

"Do you feel like talking?"

"I guess; nurse, they called me Holly. But I don't know who I am. My mind is blank. Can you tell me what happened to me?" she asked the white-capped woman.

Nurse Lurner gave Holly the little information that she knew, that she came in by ambulance late the afternoon before, with a serious head injury.

"That's gotta be what they're calling it with the wounded soldiers, a concussion."

Holly paused, feeling confusion whirling in her mind, "Where was I when I got hurt?"

"The city library; I now know that you work there, part time."

"What's my name?"

"Holly Schoner."

"Dear God, I've never heard that name before. My mind, memories, are not there."

"Holly, I'm getting the doctor; he knows more than I do."

"OK."

Holly looked around the ward, seeing women of all ages in beds.

"I don't know who I am, but something in my brain says all this equipment, looks old, the beds, everything, and the nurse wears a strange white hat and she's dressed all in white. God, please help me."

The doctor returned after a few minutes, "The nurse's filled me in. It sounds like you have temporary memory loss, Holly. It happens with head injuries."

"When do you think I'll start remembering?"

She watched his eyes for clues as he spoke.

"Don't know that," he shook his head, "each brain heals differently, and we think memory may come from different parts of the brain. You have both a front and back injury to your brain."

"What'll you tell those people who were here at my bed?"

"That you've lost your memory, that you don't recognize people, or circumstances of your home and life."

"Is it possible for you to tell me about me?"

"Of course, I've been your doctor since you were a wee one. You are Holly Schoner, 19, a graduate of Riverdawn High School two years ago. You are married to the tall blonde young man who kissed you. His name is Jake. You have a daughter, about a year and a half old, Maggie. I delivered her. Oh, our town is Riverdawn, Iowa, off Highway 18, in the middle of the state."

"What year is it?"

"1946, today is Friday, December 13, it's afternoon. We need you to drink a lot of water. And I'm ordering gelatin for you. You haven't eaten for a day."

"Can I go home, but I don't know where that is?"

Holly began to cry. The doctor held her hand and stayed with her.

"I'll send you home, in a little while. First I need to talk to your family. You are going to need a lot of help, until your memory returns."

Interstate Power and Light let Jake off so he could return to the hospital. Tom finished his mailman's route and joined Jake. Jake's mom, Dee, came to the hospital. Dr. Abram sat with the three of them in a corner of the waiting room.

"Her amnesia (that's loss of memory) concerns us; it's the head blows that are probably causing this. Holly doesn't know who she is. Before you came we gave her a mirror. She gasped as she looked into the mirror and said she never saw that person before. We're sending her home, thinking that's the best place for her to regain her memory, in the home where she's loved, and with people who will have to learn to work with her until her memory returns."

"Can she read, write?"

"Yes, she's shown us she can, so her education brain patterns, they seem not to be affected, well, at this time. It's people, places, time, everything else, it's a memory gone now."

The doctor saw tears in everyone's eyes. He heard silence as the family began to process what happened to their Holly.

"Patience, we're going to have to have patience, as Holly's brain heals, isn't that right, doc?"

"Anger at her inabilities will get the family nowhere."

"What about Maggie?"

"The family will have to see how she gets along with her daughter."

ഇ

Jake drove Holly and his mom to the couple's home. Dee went ahead into the home to let Ellie and Maggie know that Holly's head hurt. The pain pill wore off as they left the hospital. Holly had enough pain pills for several days. Then she had an appointment on Monday at the doctor's office to remove the stitches in both the front and back of her head.

Holly held tight to Jake's arm as they walked up to the front porch. She looked around at the snowy front yard. And the house, she never saw before.

"Uh, I'm so frightened, I've no knowledge of any of this. You're Jake, right?"

"That's right, Holly, I'm your husband, and your daughter is Maggie. I know you don't feel good, but maybe you could give her a hug. Ellie says she really misses you."

"I will make sure I hug her. It's not her fault I can't remember."

"We're going to help you, Holly, until your memory comes back."

"You have to, I know nothing. The doctor said it was 1946, is that right?"

"Yes, it is, actually it is Friday, December 13."

"A Friday the 13th?"

Holly felt a flash of pain sock her head, as if she knew something about that date.

"Yes, let's go in."

She smelled chicken as it fried on the kitchen stove. She felt the warmth of the home and the yummy-smelling chicken.

A pretty blonde woman came to her, "Holly, I'm Ellie, I'm your mom. And on the floor there with her blocks is your daughter, our granddaughter, Maggie. Would you like to say hello to her before you go and lie down?"

"I would."

Jake took her coat and the bag she carried in. She got down on her knees and spoke out, "Oh Abby, it's so good to see you."

She reached out her arms to her daughter as the little girl got up and moved to Holly.

"Maggie, I'm Maggie, Mommy."

"Maggie?"

She hugged her daughter.

"I missed you, sweet girl." She turned and looked up to Ellie and Jake. "Oh I need help. My head hurts, please take Abby, I mean Maggie."

Jake helped her get up as she began to cry.

She whispered to the adults, "Nothing makes sense, you are all strangers to me, I'm so sorry," she shook her head. "I need to lie down and take a pain pill. And I don't want to scare this little girl."

"Cookie, Mommy?"

She heard the small voice as Maggie walked up to her mother.

"Oh, I am hungry, please could I have a cookie and something to drink with my pill?"

Jake guided her to their bedroom. With his arm helping she lay down. He covered her with a blanket. Ellie brought warm milk and a cookie. She sat up and swallowed the pain pill with milk. She took several bites of the soft tasty sugar cookie.

He gazed down at Holly, "Sweetie, I'll let you rest. Your mom will stay for as long as it takes, to take care of Maggie and you. I hope I'll be here for the weekend. But I get called at crazy times and this is my weekend to respond."

She handed him the glass and part of the cookie she didn't eat. Holly's eyes closed; the pain pill began to help her.

Her parents sat at the small kitchen table with Jake and his parents, Greg and Dee.

"We'll handle this one day at a time, Mom and Dad, Ellie and Tom."

"We're here for you, son; we know you get called out, a lot now after hours and on weekends, with the snow season, the snow and ice on the lines."

"That's absolutely correct," Ellie and Tom added. "We all live within six blocks of each other. And we have the telephone for communication."

"Yes, thank goodness for the telephone."

Greg and Dee rose to leave.

"Keep us informed; whatever we can do."

Holly woke. She looked around the bedroom. She saw a streetlight shining in from outside.

"It's dark; how long have I been asleep?"

She got up slow and walked out to go to the bathroom. After that she looked in the mirror.

"Who am I?" she asked the reflection in the mirror, a blonde woman with hair that curled above her shoulders and blue eyes, the skin around her eyes blackened by the fall she took. She pressed her hand on the gauze bandage on her forehead.

"It hurts," she nodded her head, watching herself in the mirror. She washed her hands at the sink with soap that had a pleasant smell. She turned and saw the closed shelving across from the sink.

"Maybe stuff?"

She found a brush and brushed her hair, being careful of the small taped wound on the back of her head. She raised her arms and noted the smell of perspiration.

"Ick, gosh I smell, but I need to go out and see these folks."

She made her way with slow steps to the light. She looked around at a living room that led into a dining area and then a kitchen

"Sweetie, you're up, come join us at the kitchen table. We saved you a plate, fried chicken breast, mashed potatoes and a roll."

"Thanks," she smiled to Jake.

"I gave Maggie her bath, read to her, and she's asleep now. You did such a great job of training her to have her bath, be read to, and go to bed at the correct time, and to go to sleep," Ellie smiled to her daughter.

"And she rarely wakes up in the middle of the night, just a couple of times, when she got sick," Jake added.

"I'll eat and drink more milk. While I'm eating, please tell me stuff I must know to survive. Uuummm, this chicken is tender and delicious, please talk to me."

"Holly, you and me," he touched her shoulder and smiled to her, "we been really good friends since our teacher decided to skip us two grades, fifth and sixth. We landed at the high school as very young 9th graders. We're childhood sweethearts, graduated from high school in May 1945, when we just turned 17. That was before the war with Japan ended in September. We got married soon after we graduated. Maggie was born in October 1945."

Holly stopped eating and wiped her lips with her cloth napkin.

"I still can do math; sorry, but I need to say this."

She looked into Jake's eyes, "We were having sex, before we got married?"

"That's right, Holly, we were, and we still are, so much in love." He patted her arm and whispered, "Maggie's just added to our love."

"Sorry, I speak out what I think; I," she paused, "I have to absorb so much. I guess I can call you Mom and Dad, uh what was your reaction when you found out about the baby?"

Ellie touched Tom's hand, "We were over the moon for you both. You don't know about this, but the war, it was devastating to us adults. You young folks took everything more in stride, but you weren't fighting in this war. All of us looked for ways to be happy, and the joy and love you two had for each other, that was happiness for us also. Look at your dad, Holly. Do you see anything different about his eyes?"

"Yes," she paused, "do you have an injury from the war?"

"I do, Holly, shrapnel took my eye."

"Did that mean you were injured, so could come home?"

"Dear Holly, that's right, that meant I got to see you and Jake graduate, get married, be with you when Maggie came, her baptism, first birthday. God took one eye from me, but He's brought me much joy."

A surge of gratefulness filled Holly's mind. She sat, quiet for a little while. "Gosh, and Mom, you help with Maggie?"

"I do, on Tuesday and Thursday afternoons, so you can work your little job at the library. I work at the library all day Monday, Wednesday, and Friday."

"The nurse said I got the head injury at the library."

"That's right, a shelf took you down."

"Oh my."

She shook her head in slow motion, "Nothing, I have no memory," she thought.

"What do you do, Dad?"

"Mailman for the postal service, serving our town of Riverdawn."

"Jake, uh, what do you do?"

"I'm with the power company. I spend time going up and down power poles all over the area, fixing downed electrical, and sometimes phone lines. And in good weather, we change out lines, transformers, that electrical kind of stuff."

Holly teared up, "That sounds," she stopped and cried out, "like incredibly dangerous work, ice and snow, the cold, oh Jake."

She began to tremble and cry, "This's too much. I need to lie down. But I feel dirty. I need to shower. Mom, uh, can you possibly stay tonight?"

Ellie touched her daughter's shoulder, "Tonight, and for as long as I'm needed by my family."

"I'll say goodnight to you now, Holly; I'll bed down on the comfy couch and take a quick shower in the morning. I have my work clothes out for then. I am so happy," Jake paused, "that you are home with us."

She watched him come close to her. He gave her a gentle kiss on top of her head.

#### ℘

Holly eased out of bed. The sun shone into the bedroom window. She noticed blue sky and puffy clouds. And she heard the sounds of chatter from the kitchen.

"Coffee, oh I smell coffee. My daughter, Maggie, oh why do I keep almost saying Abby, and my mom, uh, is Ellie. My head feels better, but the doctor asked me to take the pills until I go to get stitches out."

She found a robe in the closet where both her and Jake's clothes hung. She went next door to the bathroom. She saw that skin around her eyes seemed less dark. She felt her breasts and touched her tummy.

"I may have had a baby, but my breasts aren't droopy and my tum's flat. I must have taken care of myself after the baby came. Or maybe I didn't gain much weight. I need to ask."

Holly walked with a slow pace into the kitchen.

"Good morning, Mom, and sweet little," she paused, "Maggie."

She kissed Maggie on top of her head and heard Maggie say, "Moning."

Maggie sat in a wooden high-chair, spooning a mushy tan cereal into her mouth.

Holly shook her head to her mom, "Jake?""

"He got called, early."

"Saturday?"

"Oh, daughter, he's called out to his job day and night, 24 hours a day. That's one weekend a month, on his work schedule."

"The other three weeks?"

"Monday through Friday, but that can change, especially in winter."

She felt a cramp through her tummy as she spoke out, "Golly, isn't that terribly hard for him?"

"He loves his job, been doing it since summer of his junior year of high school. He's so tall, those long legs. And our men were gone, fighting in the war, so many young men in high school got called up to do very adult jobs."

"I will need you very much, Mom. I took a pain pill so I'm doing better than when I first got up. What I know is that I work at the library on Tuesday and Thursday afternoons, someone said that. So you take care of Maggie then. What is my life like; what do I do during the day besides take care of Maggie?"

"Besides being a mom you do dishes, cook meals, do the wash and iron, sweep and vacuum your home, clean the bathroom, help Jake with the yard and shovel snow in the winter . You have a '40 Ford that stays in the garage that's next to the house, unless you need to use the car. You shop for groceries and other supplies you all need."

"How does Jake get to work?"

"He gets picked up. That helps at nighttime and over weekends because the power company uses vehicles that get around good in the snow. That way they can always pick up the workers they need to do the special work. We have power outages, and snapped power lines, and sometimes snapped power poles."

"Ah, the snow and ice," she nodded to her mom.

"Yes, winters often are difficult."

Holly sat for a moment, her mind whirling with thoughts of difficult winter.

"Uh, it's the middle of December, uh, it's the Christmas season. What do people do for Christmas?"

"Our country is feeling better about itself; we talk in our family about having a Christmas tree again this year. Last Christmas, December of 1945, our men were still coming home from the war. Folks had trees last year, but it was a very hard time for the families who lost loved ones, who had men come home with such serious injuries, both in body and mind."

"So, did Jake and I have a tree last year?"

"A tiny tree, Maggie was very small. But this year perhaps a larger tree, for her to look at and enjoy; she walks very well now."

Ellie saw a wide-eyed look on her daughter's face and a shake of her head.

"We'll look around to see if there are any decorations from the tree last year."

"Mom, you, you must teach me about the stove, and I saw a washing machine, with a name Bendix, off the kitchen. I do not know how to use it. I need your help in seeing what is in the refrigerator and freezer, stuff to fix. I sense I know how to cook, but cook what?"

Holly sat down and began sobbing, "I don't know anything, about me, about you and the baby, about this world I live in."

Ellie poured her daughter a cup of coffee and fixed her a bowl of warm cereal.

"The brown sugar makes this taste good; what's the cereal?"

"Oats."

"What's, uh, Maggie eating?"

"Same as you, oats."

"She uses her spoon really good, not messy."

"And you almost have her potty trained," Ellie patted her daughter on the arm.

"Uh, that's good?"

"It's a bit unusual at 15 months, but Holly, Maggie is a very smart little girl. In her little voice, she can recite certain parts of books."

"Did I read a lot to her?"

"Yes, from the time she came home from the hospital. You and Jake read to her during the day and before bed."

"She must follow along with the words on the page of the book, recognizing words?"

"Yes, she does that. And I know you talk to her about the story, and for her favorite books, she reads a little to you."

"From somewhere I seem to know about coloring; does she have color books and stuff to color with?"

"Yes, they're called crayons, and she has a little artist's area in her room, on her bookshelf."

"Paints?"

"Yes, she paints with watercolors. We have several pieces of her artwork at our home."

"Little friends?"

"Yes, Holly, your friend from high school, Cindy, and her daughter, Peggy, they come over here part of a morning, usually once a week. Peggy and Maggie were born just a few days apart; they're both 15 months old."

"Uh, don't know how to ask this, why did us teens get married so young?"

"Yes, it happened here, as well as I think other places. We celebrated our new lives, without a war, and young people celebrated, bringing on another generation. Holly, we lost so many men in the war. It's kind of a regeneration of ourselves."

"Yes, I guess that's right. But something in her brain brought on a quick sharp pain to her head and a thought, "So young."

The rest of that Saturday Ellie explained the workings of Holly's home, the stove, and stove burners, and how to light the gas oven. Together they washed clothes in the washing machine. Eventually Holly got the hang of how to send the clothes through the ringer to get the water out of the clothes. They hung up the clothes in the basement furnace room in the winter to air dry.

"We were so lucky to find you and Jake a reconditioned washer for your home. During the war, only war production took place."

"What did that mean, Mom?"

"No cars, no washing machines, nothing that we all considered essential to our lives before the war happened, got made. Our country was totally committed to winning the war for us and for our allies."

"Sounds like everyone learned how to fix up broken stuff."

"That was it."

"A car, in the garage, is it OK?"

"Oh, yes, we gave it to Jake in high school when we got hold of another '40 Ford for us. Jake's dad spent the war overseas."

"So, everyone did pretty much jobs, men's jobs."

"I drove road graders, old stuff, to keep the roads plowed in the winter. We're just beginning to see the production of everything our country really needs. One of the biggest things are tires. We all had to learn to change flat tires."

"The tires, really old?"

"Unbelievable, what we used to drive on, throughout the war. So rubber production, it's a huge need."

Ellie made out menus for Holly, of the meals she knew of that Jake and Maggie ate. They went through the cupboards, the refrigerator with a top freezer box to find food for meals.

Holly created a list after she had success putting Maggie down for a nap. Ellie got ready to go to the grocery store by car.

"Jake'll pay you back. How do we handle money?"

"Jake gives you money for groceries. Some things people pay for by check. Oh, and the telephone, you haven't been up when the wall phone rings. You are on a party line."

"What does that mean?"

"Two families share one phone line. If a call comes in and it's one ring, that's you and Jake. If a call comes in that's a double ring, that's for the other family."

"Good idea to answer the phone as quick as I can?"

"Yes, and if you pick up the phone when you want to make a call, you may hear voices. That means the phone is in use by the other family on your line. Please respect their privacy."

"I certainly will hang up. Uh, what do I do to call someone?"

"A telephone operator will answer and ask you for a number. And here's where you keep the phone book." She pointed to a lower cabinet. "Just give the operator the name or the number, she'll transfer you to that number."

"Please go, Mom, I will lie down and listen for Maggie. I'm tired, but I want to save my pill for tonight. Something tells me I need to stop taking a pill, to see how I do without it."

Holly watched her mom wave to her as she left for the store. She lay down on the bed in their bedroom. She closed her eyes and rested. After 20 minutes she roused to check on Maggie, who woke up and lay singing in her crib.

"You are such a happy little girl," Holly smiled to her daughter. As she started to change Maggie a sharp pain hit her head. It had something to do with the cloth diaper, a clean one she placed on Maggie along with rubber pants over. She rinsed out the dirty diaper and flushed the stool. Then the diaper went into a small covered pail in her daughter's bedroom.

"Well, Maggie, mom said you were starting to be potty trained. That's good," she looked down to her, "because cloth diapers, hard work to keep you in clean diapers. One of these days."

Maggie looked up to her mom, "Potty in stul."

"That's right, you really understand. You are smart."

Holly took Maggie's hand as they went from the bedroom through the home to the kitchen.

"Smart," she heard her daughter say.

"Your grandma will be here soon; what do you like to do in the afternoon after your nap?

Maggie pointed to her high-chair and said, "Milk, apsauce."

"Can do."

Holly helped her daughter into the high-chair and poured her milk. She found a jar of applesauce in the refrigerator and gave Maggie a dish of that. She got herself coffee and a part of a cookie and sat down near to her daughter at the kitchen table. Once again she watched her daughter use her spoon and put the applesauce in her mouth without spilling any or messing up her face.

"You are careful when you eat, Maggie."

She nodded to her mom and asked, "Moosik?"

"You mean music, on the radio?"

"Yes, Mommy."

Holly found the radio, a stand up piece of furniture in the living room. She looked at the dial on the front to turn it on. She saw other various knobs. Holly stopped the dial at a station that played what sounded like Christmas music.

"Nice music?"

Maggie nodded, "Nice."

Just then Holly's mom arrived with groceries. Holly listened as Ellie explained about the food, what needed to be refrigerated, to be put in the freezer compartment at the top of the refrigerator, and what could remain out, to be put away in cupboards for storage.

"Thank you, this matches the menus we set up. Tonight I will cook my first meal; I'm glad Maggie likes macaroni, then put the creamy cheese with it to make a meal for all of us."

"Right now, macaroni and cheese is just about her favorite meal."

"I must remember that."

All the while they were working in the kitchen, Holly kept an eye on Maggie, who played on the living room rug with her blocks that Holly helped her bring out from her bedroom. Holly noticed how Maggie kept her bedroom neat, putting away toys before she brought out new toys to the living room.

Holly thought, "Things are messy, the kitchen counters, things not put away all over the home. I need to fix that. My daughter has better housekeeping abilities than it looks like I have."

Holly touched her mom's shoulder after they sipped coffee, standing in the kitchen.

"I got it; I have to go on by myself, with Maggie's help. She knows so much. Mom, go home, you have three days of work at home, been with Maggie since my accident on Thursday. Today's Saturday, and thank you for all you've done for us. Tell me what happens tomorrow, Sunday, that's the 15th. I have the newspaper and a calendar to help me."

"Sunday we all go to church, Jake's folks, us, you, Jake and Maggie. Maggie spends her time with the toddlers in their Sunday School class; they do basic simply play times, with God in mind. And the little ones, they're excited about Baby Jesus coming."

"This week, maybe Jake can take Maggie; I need a little time Sunday morning to get my mind around this future of mine. I try to read the paper, little bits of information. It gives me such a helpless feeling, but then I read something that seems to be back in my brain somewhere. It makes me feel a little better."

"And then Sunday after church, we gather, take turns at each other's homes, a kind of potluck, and celebrate another week together."

"Not sure, potluck?"

"We each bring a part of the meal that's decided ahead of time."

"Been doing that long?"

"Pretty much since you and Jake married. Greg, Jake's dad, wasn't home from the war yet; it didn't end in Europe until after you married. But the three families made a decision, to be grateful for God allowing us all to be together."

Holly smiled to her mom, "That had to be so wonderful, when Greg got to come home."

"Yes, we were all together, finally, and then Maggie joined us. We are so blessed, Holly. God gave us back our men."

"Dad, horribly injured; he was lucky to keep the one eye."

"He also suffered the shrapnel grazing his head, with the piece taking his eye. So he suffered headaches, the trauma, like you're having. But he came out of it, headaches stopped, as we're praying the headaches will stop for you."

"I understand the meals together; how much that means to all of you."

"I'm sure we'll stop doing this most Sundays. But for now, especially with Christmas coming, it's something we like to do."

"What about this Sunday?"

"We'll hold off, until you're feeling more yourself."

"But, by Christmas," Holly affirmed to her mom.

"Oh, yes."

Maggie put her blocks away and brought a book for Holly to read to her.

"I'll leave; I want you three to be together when Jake gets home."

"Thank you, for everything," she paused, "Mom."

Her mom captured Holly's wide smile, "My pleasure, dear daughter.

# 2

7 a.m., Sunday, December 17, 2006, Porttown, Iowa

Evan Huan stood next to Kate's bed in her neuro ward room. The odor of antiseptic almost took his breath away. He touched her hand and bent his head.

"Kate, I want you to wake up; I miss you, and I didn't sleep at all last night, just flipped around. But I prayed, like I'm praying now, lots of *Lord's Prayer.* You got hit so hard, landing on your forehead with the force of the wood on the back of your head. It looked pretty bad. Then I remembered what you always told me about your being hard-headed. Yeah, so stubborn, I'm not kidding, maybe it'll help you now. I love you. The play, so awesome, hey, we got a write up in today's paper. Yeah, I looked at the paper; it comes early and I was already up. I think *High School Musical* will end up being a super popular play to perform," he nodded as he finished speaking.

Evan gazed at her face, the butterfly bandages keeping the cut in her forehead in place. He teared up as he looked at the blackened skin around her eyes and the greenish color of her forehead.

"I'm going to mass at 8:30. I sure need to talk to God. Maybe I can do that there. Right now my mind just spins around, seeing scenes from the play with you and me. Christmas's coming. Your mom and dad, yeah, I talked to them late last night. It'll help us all when the results of the MRI are given to your family by the docs. Everyone wants you to wake up."

He leaned over and kissed her cheek, whispering, "Wake up, Gabriella, it's Troy speakin'."

He walked out of her room, "Maybe that'll help her, hearing me as Troy, speaking to her, as her character, Gabriella."

Two hours later Kate's parents, David and Ann, watched over her. And they learned from the doctor that the MRI results were inconclusive. Whatever would happen, it would take time. They were told to be patient and to go home. They indicated to staff they would return later in the afternoon. Her care nurse mentioned that Evan came by to see their daughter.

As they left, they held hands until they got to the lobby.

"Evan, he's such a fine young man, so concerned about Kate."

"Honey, he loves our daughter."

Ann started to tear up, "So blessed, we've been so blessed with Kate."

David held her tight as they stood near the Christmas tree in the hospital lobby.

"Yes, she is loved, and she loves."

It hit David then, a dreaded question that continued to swirl in his head, "What if she doesn't wake up?"

His tears started then. They held on to each other as they cried, walking from the hospital to their car.

&infin;

Dinner time, Saturday evening, December 14, 1946

"How are you feeling?"

Jake looked down, smiling to Holly.

"I didn't take a pill all day. I'll take one before bed to help me to sleep, but I want to go off the pain help tomorrow. My mind's in a big fog, trying to learn as much as I can."

"Something smells good."

"My first attempt at fixing a meal. Mom says it's Maggie's favorite."

"Ah, macaroni and cheese."

"And Maggie told me that when I started cooking."

"I'll shower and then let's have dinner."

"Yes, Maggie needs to eat."

"How are you two getting along?"

"A delight, she is really a delight, very smart and knows our routine, and she senses I am not the person I was before the accident. I talked to her about my accident. She seems to understand my hesitancy about everything, so she really helps me."

"We have always talked to her in adult language, Holly."

After Jake showered they sat together having dinner.

"Yummy," Maggie pointed to her bowl of mac and cheese.

"Would you like more?"

"Peaz."

Jake put several more spoonfuls of food in Holly's bowl.

"Why don't you go give Maggie her bath and I will wash the dishes."

"Yes, that will give me a chance to do that task with her."

After her bath Jake sat with Holly and Maggie at the comfy couch. They each read a part of a story to her.

Maggie pointed out a picture and often said a word or two from the story.

"Sleepy time?"

Maggie nodded. Together her parents walked to her bedroom, each one holding her hand. Holly changed her.

Jake came forward and picked her up.

"Goodnight, sweet girl," he kissed her forehead and laid her down.

"Does she take anything to bed?"

"A favorite blankie she holds close to her when she goes to sleep."

"I see it's in her bed. Then we check her, is that right?"

"Before we go to sleep, usually you check her. She's such a good little girl at night."

"That's what my mom says. Do we keep her door open?"

"Yes, a little bit, and she has a back alley light as her kind of light, coming in to her room through the thin curtain. Let's sit back on the couch, Holly."

"I feel very uncomfortable; I don't know you, Jake. And I know that's hard for you. Let's talk, you can fill me in on what's coming up, a helpless feeling, with Christmas coming."

"Tomorrow I'll take Maggie to church, if I don't get called."

"Mom says she likes being with the other little children."

"She sure does, and she likes seeing both sets of grandparents after church. But this week we won't have a Sunday dinner with everyone."

"Jake, I don't know you," Holly shook her head to him.

"And I'm trying, but I'm still a stranger in my home."

"A little bit at a time, I would like to sleep in bed with you tonight. This has been the longest time that we've ever been apart. I know, understand completely that you are not ready for an intimate relationship with me. What do you think about that?"

"Yes, I would like that. Maybe the comfort of having you nearby will shake something lose with my lack of my memory."

"Perhaps, let's plan Christmas tomorrow. That will be fun. Would you like to think about a Christmas tree?"

Jake watched her give him a wide smile, a smile he never saw before. And her blackened eyes had a sparkle in the blue corneas. He remembered his wife as not being a smiler, more keeping her thoughts to herself.

"I like how you smile, Holly, and your sparkle in your eyes. That's a change I really like."

Holly giggled, "I guess this is the new me, OK?"

"I'll turn on the radio; there's lots of Christmas music starting to be played. I know you used to love having the radio on."

"Please do that, and Jake, I would like an hour, to shower, and to make some kind of order, what I call it. I noticed how neat Maggie is with her room. I'd like to do that for several rooms in the house."

"I'll start with our closet. I have a tendency to throw stuff in the closet corner. I'll hang up stuff that's OK. You may have a few things of mine for a wash."

"Mom taught me how to manage the wringer washer. It's work."

"Sweetie, that's what you're learning, most everything is work. But it wasn't long ago that women did the wash on a wash board."

Holly shook her head, got up and went to the kitchen where she began to put away the dishes Jake washed and let air dry.

"I want my kitchen counters clear, gives the look of order. And it gives me a chance to see where everything goes."

Jake worked in their clothes closet.

"When you're done there, please put your dirty clothes in the hamper. Then maybe we can look to see where the Christmas decorations are located."

Holly continued to look in closets. To her surprise she found a box on the top shelf of the guest bedroom with a sign Christmas Decorations.

"Jake, oh joy," she held the box as she found him looking through a box of his stuff on the shelf of their own closet. He looked up to her, again seeing that wide smile, so new to him.

"I am glad; if you will take the box to the kitchen table, we'll look through it, tomorrow a tree?"

"That would be wonderful."

They went through the box, Jake explaining about the decorations.

"This one is Maggie's; we decided to add a decoration a year for her."

"How great, soon we will be able to explain the decorations to her."

"Christmas, it will be a wonderful holiday for all of us."

"I hope to be back with you; my memory to return, that will be my Christmas wish."

They each stood up from the table. Jake held out his arms to her. With a little hesitancy she moved into his arms and put her arms around him.

"You are my sweet one, Holly, named for a holiday plant that happens to grow in a lot of places and during a lot of the year."

"I am still scared, of you, of this life I am thrust into."

"Go ahead and shower; I'll read and wait for you. You mentioned that your forehead is itchy. Let's take off the bandage and see how the stitches look. It'll give us both a chance to see your progress. The blackening around your eyes, it's going away."

"Then it will be good news, depending on how the stitches look. And the stitches in the back of my head, they're starting to itch."

"That is good; Monday will be a very good day for you, getting your stitches out and seeing how your progress is with your memory."

Holly showered and put on short pajamas that she found in one of her drawers. She sat on the side of the bed as Jake used caution in removing the dressing on her forehead.

"Oh, Holly, the stitches look good, like doc said he made careful stitches, so you would not scar, after the initial redness of the wound goes away."

"And the back of my head, I can't wait to wash my hair, after those stitches come out. Some of it must have been a bloody mess after the hit."

"The hospital staff, they really cleaned the wound up. There is no blood to be seen."

"Let me go look at myself in the bathroom mirror."

Holly stood in front of the mirror. In the reflection she saw a blonde woman with stitches that seemed clean, no oozing of infection. She prayed the back stitches were the same way.

"Oh, my hair needs washing, uh when do I wash it, and how do I get it dry? I need to look for stuff for my hair."

A sharp pain stabbed her head as she spoke the question.

"What is going on, the stab of pain, is something coming back to me, and the pain makes me aware of it?"

"I checked on Maggie. She's sleeping."

"Thanks, I eventually will get the routine down."

She got into bed next to this tall man, Jake.

"This will take me awhile, being near to you in this bed."

"And I don't want to scare you; I see a glint of fear in your eyes, as you look at me. Let's go to sleep, time Holly, time."

"Yes."

He turned off the bed lamp next to his side of the bed.

"Goodnight, sweet Holly."

"Goodnight."

She woke to find that he lay close to her. Holly looked out the window through the thin curtain.

"Oh God, you bring me the sunshine; please help me have a good day, with my new family."

When she returned from the bathroom, she saw Jake turned to the side, fast asleep.

"He hasn't gotten called, yet," she thought. "Maybe he will be able to go to church with Maggie and our family."

She went to the closet and brought out the outfit, pants, shirt, and sweater that she wanted to wear for the day.

"All these clothes look strange," she whispered as she dressed. Holly heard Maggie singing in her crib, and she heard the mommy call.

Within a few minutes Holly figured out the diaper and clothes routine. Together they walked from the bedroom through the living room to the kitchen.

"Where should we put the Christmas tree, Maggie?"

The little girl turned a complete circle and pointed to a place in the room. Then she went to the spot.

"Tree," she announced.

"Why thank you, I think that place will work great."

"Toast peaz, Mommy."

Holly found the toaster and toasted a piece of bread for each of them.

"Jelly on toast?"

"Pwez."

Holly cut the toast in four pieces after she applied a little jelly. Maggie reminded her of her bib.

She nodded to Maggie, "You want to keep your Sunday outfit nice and clean."

Maggie smiled to her mom and nodded her head.

Holly and her daughter ate oatmeal Holly cooked. She added brown sugar.

"Delicious," she said to Maggie.

Maggie gave her a questioning look and said, "Dewishus."

"Yes, it means tastes very good."

Jake stood in the middle of the living room, dressed in a dark suit and blue tie for church. He felt a warmth spread up from his chest to his head, "Holly, I think, is coming back. She sure is good with Maggie, now really comfortable with our daughter."

He gazed with amazement as they talked and giggled as they ate.

"Good morning, you two."

He patted Holly on the shoulder and gave Maggie a kiss on the top of her head.

"Moning, Daddy."

Then she took another spoonful of her oatmeal.

She pointed to it and looked up to her dad, "Dewishus."

"Maggie, that's a big word. Where did you learn that?"

Maggie pointed to Holly, "Mommy."

"Did you make my coffee?" Jake asked.

Holly felt a sharp pain sear her head.

From somewhere in her brain she spoke out, "Please make your coffee. We have been eating."

What he asked bothered Holly as she thought about him not making coffee. And last night he acted like he didn't often do dishes. She needed to ask her mom or someone about what men actually did to help with chores and child care. She also remembered he stood next to her when she changed Maggie, but he didn't offer to change her diaper. Then she remembered that they told her it was 1946.

"In my brain, I'm starting to feel like I'm in some kind of time warp. That blow to my head, it's seriously affecting me."

And Holly noticed that Jake did not make any coffee. He also did not eat any breakfast. She finished her breakfast and helped Maggie wipe her hands and face. Jake sat on the couch reading the newspaper. Maggie crawled up next to him.

"Read, pwez."

Jake sat her on his lap and pointed out the words as he read to her. The story was about the different churches in Riverdawn and when they would have their Christmas services.

"Maggie, Baby Jesus is coming in several weeks."

Maggie clapped her hands.

"Let's ask Mommy to help get you ready for church."

Maggie walked with Holly to the bedroom.

"Maggie, do you take a bag with you, with a diaper and cloths to wipe you?"

Maggie nodded and produced a bag that she handed to Holly.

"Why thank you, let's put several diapers, and another rubber pants, in case, another outfit."

When they were all packed up, Maggie carried the bag to her dad.

"We'll see you after church; I'll stop by my folks so they can say hello to Maggie. They decided not to go to church today. Next week, though, we'll all attend. You're doing so well."

He came to Holly and gave her a hug. He picked up Maggie, and they left the home for the detached garage. Holly watched him open the garage door with one hand, while holding Maggie and her bag in his other arm.

"The garage door must not be too heavy. I want to drive the car today. I know I must drive this car. I have so much to learn. Oh, Holly, whoever I am, this is so hard. And I cannot fake what is happening. Here is the life I am living. I am so glad Christmas is coming."

Holly got down on her knees after she made the bed in their bedroom.

"God, I am asking for your help. Frustrating, lost, sad, please guide me."

She lay her head to the side of the bed and cried. She crawled up and lay on top of the bed and fell asleep. Holly jerked awake and looked at the ticking clock in their bedroom. She saw that 15 minutes passed.

She walked from the bedroom. For a moment she felt complete disorientation.

"Where am I and who am I?"

She took deep breaths, in and out, and in several minutes she regained her composure.

"I wonder if I learned that when I did drama in high school?"

Then she made coffee. It seemed to be a bone of contention with Jake. Holly resolved to try to get along, to make coffee each morning, for starters. She remembered how her mom talked about how precious coffee was during the war. One cup a day was the rule for Americans coffee drinkers.

"Stop being a baby, Holly; I have a baby, who right now seems more grown up than I am. Feeling sorry for myself will get me nowhere."

She found the vacuum where her mom showed her. She vacuumed the rugs in the living room, hallway, and three bedrooms. Then she swept the kitchen floor with the broom hanging in the hall closet.

"The garage, what do I need to know about that place?"

She got a coat from the front closet and went out the back door. The side door to the garage opened easy and she turned on the light. She saw a small workbench area in front of where the car parked.

"Jake, he keeps this nice and neat, his stuff he works on. A rotary lawn mower sits on the other side of the garage, up toward the front. Good for him, more of an incentive for me to clean up."

After she left the garage she went to the basement. It was one large unfinished room. She smelled a musty odor, then saw a water heater and a forced-air furnace with ducts all over the basement ceiling. She felt the clothes she and her mom hung up the day before. They were dry, but wrinkly.

"Sending stuff through the wringer on the washing machine sure messes them up. I gotta find an iron and an ironing board."

She tried to remember where her mom showed her. She couldn't absorb all the things she had to learn in that short time. Holly shook her head as she trudged up the steps from the basement. She tried the guest bedroom closet.

"I got lucky; here's where the iron and stuff are."

After she looked in the clothes hamper, she decided.

"I gotta wash every week day; to keep up with diapers and my and Jake's clothes, being a mom, a heck of a lot of work. Whew, God, and your helpers, I need your advice."

Jake and Maggie arrived home for lunch, soup and sandwiches. Maggie ran to her mom, "Mommy, bell."

"This is wonderful, Maggie, a bell for the Christmas tree we're getting?"

"Yes, Mommy."

They hugged and Holly examined the bell, made from stiff silver paper. A pipe cleaner helped the bell hang, and the best part was the jingle of an actual bell that was attached to the bottom of the pipe cleaner.

"You made this, with a little help in Sunday School?"

Maggie smiled to her mom and nodded, "Hep."

Jake stood, watching the interaction of his wife and daughter.

"It's swell to see them together, getting along so good," he thought. "Whatever happened, it seems Holly is comfortable and confident, with Maggie, like she's had some experience with little ones before. I love seeing this, thank you God."

After lunch Maggie went down for her nap. When she awoke, the family got into their car and went to the Grayson Christmas tree lot, on the far end of Riverdawn's main street. They looked for a four-foot tree. And Holly met several families who were acquainted with them. They asked how she was doing and she told them that her head still hurt sometimes and that she was having a loss of memory. The folks looked at the stitches on her forehead and saw her blackened forehead and eyes. They all gave each other Christmas greetings and wishes for Holly getting back to her old self.

Jake sat the tree in the spot in the living room that Maggie suggested to Holly earlier. They scooted furniture away to give the handsome tree enough space. Maggie helped by telling her parents where the tree ornaments should go. When they finished, Jake picked Maggie up so she could place strands of silver tinsel all around the top of the tree.

"Mommy, would you like to put tinsel around the rest of the tree?"

With reluctance Holly placed a few strands of the tinsel on the rest of the tree. She thought to herself, "Looks pretty bad, wonder who decided tinsel makes the tree look better?"

As with everything she could not remember tree decorating. But something in her mind told about the look. She knelt near the tree as Maggie came to her.

"Petty tree, Mommy."

"Yes, Maggie, you helped us make the tree look very pretty."

&#8450;&#8450;

"OK, Jake, I see a clutch, brake, and gas pedals on the floor. But the gear shift, it is not in the middle of the car, between the seats. Where are the gears, and we sit on one long seat?"

"The gear shift lever is here on the steering column."

He held his long fingered hand over her right hand as he showed her the gears, neutral, and reverse.

"You understand the clutch?"

"I do."

Holly backed the car out of the garage, with Jake holding Maggie. They drove around the neighborhood, and down the main streets of their town until Holly felt comfortable with the gears and shifting. Plus she started getting familiar with the streets. Jake showed her the emergency brake, the lights, hood, and trunk and how to get into them.

"Uh, how long have I been driving?"

"We started when we were 14; we got a driver's license a little later. The war effort, we all were doing all kinds of jobs."

"Young men, driving very early because they had men's jobs, from the time they could do them."

"That's right, Holly, but girls also learned to drive early; we were a nation at war, and without men, except the elderly and boys in elementary and junior high school and those who could not serve for many reasons."

"Your mom, Jake, what does she do?"

"She's a seamstress, full time, works out of the sewing room in our home. Most everyone sewed some clothes at home during the war. She produces dresses for all occasions and suits, women's and men's. People tell me she does beautiful work."

"And during the war, my mom drove a machine, a road grader."

"Mom delivered milk, to homes, schools, the hospital and nursing home."

"So she drove a milk delivery truck?"

"And she could carry those metal milk cans filled with milk; she's very strong."

"Everybody, young and old, worked very hard, I understand that now."

"We did, and we all still do. And now we can produce corn for our own country. Iowa is glad for that. Grain went for the war effort."

"I'm comfortable driving now. Let's head home because my head's hurting, trying to take this all in."

When they arrived home, Holly wanted to get out and open the garage door, to see how heavy it was. She tried it and found it to be easy to pull the door up. Then she drove the car into the garage, being careful to park it directly in the middle so both sides could get out.

Jake carried Maggie in and took her to her bedroom where he helped her off with her nice coat which he hung in the closet.

"Would you like to change her, or I can," Holly offered.

Jake turned and left the room, "Something I need to do; I'll be back in a couple hours," she heard him say.

She felt her anger flare, "The guy can't help me with the baby?"

She took deep breaths and put Maggie on the change table. Then she remembered her "feel sorry for herself" incident from yesterday. She decided she would talk to Dee tomorrow morning. Jake's mom consented to drive Holly to the doctor's office for stitches removal, because Ellie worked at the library on Mondays.

"I'll read you a story, Maggie," she told her daughter as Holly put her down. Please pick the book you want and take it to the couch. I'll be there in a minute."

Holly crumpled to the rug and put her head in her hands.

"Help me, God, for the next little while, and tomorrow, at the doctor's office. Then I'll need to do a wash and iron that wrinkly stuff. I must figure out a better way to make ironing less work, maybe move the clothes to hangers as soon as I take them out of the wringer. And I need help figuring out Christmas gifts; I must ask Jake."

She got up and joined Maggie on the couch after she drank half a cup of coffee. Maggie looked through part of the story alone. Holly started at the beginning of the book.

Maggie stopped her after a page, and pointed, "Baby, Mar, Joef."

"You recognize them, Maggie, that's wonderful, "The Christ child, and his mommy and daddy."

Then Maggie pointed to her, "My Mommy," and she gave her mommy a big smile.

"I love you, Maggie."

"Wuv you."

And then she waited for Holly to continue.

℘

Dee sat in a chair opposite where Holly sat, waiting for the doctor to remove her stitches. Maggie sat in Holly's lap, and the three of them sang *Jingle Bells*. They clapped as they finished.

"That was a fun song," Holly spoke out.

She looked around the office, the smell of antiseptic and bleach very strong to her nose. The floor had bright green tile, and the furniture and appliances seemed old-fashioned to her.

Dr. Abram walked in with the nurse.

"I thought I heard folks singing a Christmas carol."

"Was that you, Maggie?"

She nodded to the doctor, "Mommy, Grama."

"Oh, they helped you?"

Maggie nodded again. Dee took Maggie as the doctor examined Holly's eyes, ears, and listened to her heart with his stethoscope.

He made quick work of the stitches both in front and behind.

"I do good stitching; once the tiny scar line fades to your skin color, no one will ever know you took the blow to the front of your head."

"Wash my hair now?"

"Yes, careful though."

"Dr. Abram, my memory is not coming back. Sometimes I have angry feelings about something that's happened to me now, as if perhaps the past is starting to reappear. But everything is so hard; everything I see, hear, I have to attack head on. I have no reference."

She started to cry, salty tears burning her eyes.

"Yes, It's a steep learning curve, but you are managing just fine, according to your mom. I called her while I was on duty yesterday, Sunday. I wanted to have another person's input, as to how you're coping."

"Maggie, she's the biggest help of all; she knows so much, I really didn't understand how much a little child knows. She certainly guides me along on quite a few things I have to do, as the responsible adult."

Holly shook her head, "But mostly I do not feel like a responsible adult; yesterday I drove the car that belongs to our family. My goodness, I didn't know where I was going, and I was trying to get used to driving the car. Shifting gears, stopping and going, and trying to see street names, and store names. It was really really hard."

Holly began to cry again.

Dr. Abram touched her arm, "I am glad you are able to cry out your frustration. I just think you need a few more days. What do you think, Dee?"

"Agree, I talk with Holly's mom, as you did. We all must learn a great deal of patience, during this time."

"I think I can find the grocery store again. That is a good thing, right?"

"Good, Holly."

&#8766;

Dee stayed for lunch, helping Holly with the meal. Afterward she read a book with Maggie and put her down for a nap. Holly washed her hair in the kitchen sink. And Dee helped her find a hair blower in the bottom cabinet of the bathroom.

"Thank you Dee, for taking me and helping me with Maggie. I feel so much better after washing my hair, like a heaviness has been removed from me. Go, I'll get my hair dry with the hair dryer. I'll have a little bit different look when my daughter sees me again." Holly laughed, "No more stringy hair."

Dee watched the wide smile on Holly's face, a sparkle in her blue eyes, the blackening around her eyes beginning to fade.

"Goodness, that's new, Holly's smile," Dee thought, "very nice."

Holly ironed, with Maggie playing with her blocks and logs on the living room rug.

Then she washed clothes, doing a much better job with the wringer washer than she did when her mom helped her. She tried her effort of hanging the clothes on hangers, smoothing them out to get rid of some of the worst wrinkles.

"Maggie, I think I will soon work out this whole washing clothes situation."

"Read, Mommy."

"Yes, we'll read with Christmas music turned on. Then I need to fix dinner for your dad, you and me."

After they read, Holly talked to Maggie about the meal.

"Tonight, it's Monday, my mom says Monday night is SPAM night."

"Uuummm, SPAM dewishous."

"Your new word, Maggie, you have a very good memory for new words."

Maggie nodded to her mom, "Good mery."

Holly looked into Maggie's eyes, "Me-mo-re."

Maggie nodded, "Me-mo-re."

"Great job, Maggie."

She smiled to her mom, "Smart."

Holly laughed at her daughter's humor and understanding of her abilities.  Then they laughed together.

℅

Holly heard the doorbell.

Maggie looked up to her mom, "Ciny, Pey."

Holly swallowed hard, took a deep breath and opened the door.  A dark-haired woman with a blonde child in her arms stood on the front step.

"Uh, hi Cindy," Holly extended her hand, "I'm Holly, and I am sorry, but I have no memory of you."

They shook hands and Holly held the door so they could come in.

They helped hang up their coats in the front closet.

Maggie took Peggy's hand, and they walked together to Maggie's room to pick out toys to bring out and play with on the living room rug.

"Oh, Holly, your home looks so nice, all picked up, and your tree, it's pretty."

"Care for coffee, uh, sit at the kitchen table while I get it ready?"

"Yes, please.  I didn't know you drank coffee?"

"I do now, and Cindy, I am not the person you knew.  I don't know myself, my memory gone, and no one knows me. I cry, am frustrated, and try to be positive, to not feel sorry for myself."

"You were my very good friend, Holly; we had almost exactly parallel lives, married our childhood sweethearts, got pregnant, got married, Peggy and Maggie are almost the same age."

Holly smiled her wide smile to the stranger who seemed to know her.

"And that wide smile, that's new, Holly, it makes you look even lovelier."

"My forehead and around my eyes, a mess, but the doc says I'll heal and not scar."

Maggie and Peggy played with the blocks and the rag dolls Maggie loved. She brought her dolls out at special times, it's what she told her mom.

"Cindy, I must ask this. Jake, he doesn't help much around the home. Is that the way men are?"

Her friend gave her a surprised look, eyebrows raised, "An example please."

"He doesn't help with diapers, acts like he doesn't do dishes, throws his clothes in the corner of our closet."

"Uh huh, I would say that may be the way it is. You've always done for him, so he expects you to do all the work."

"Is it that way at your home?"

"Yes, Holly, it is. Our guys, they've been working out of the home for so long. Has anyone talked to you about all the things young men did, while their dads and most men were away at the war?"

"Yes, I've heard about that."

"Oh Holly, our country, our women, we all had to help out, the war effort. It really galvanized our country. We still feel the joy of our men coming home.

And this cup of coffee, it's still a pleasure to have a cup. During the war, there were coffee restrictions, one cup a day. We all sacrificed, in everything we ate.

We lived on potatoes, cabbage, carrots, very little meat."

"It all went for the war effort?"

"Oh, yes."

"Last night I fixed SPAM."

Holly gave Cindy a cross-eyed look.

"What in the world is that stuff; I was afraid to ask? Jake and Maggie ate it with gusto."

Cindy giggled, "It's the kind of meat product, really what we had for years."

"It has a funny taste."

"It's a meat product."

"I talked to Maggie about it, that according to the menu my mom created for us that Monday was SPAM night. Maggie says SPAM delicious."

Cindy laughed out right, "Your daughter is such a darling; she learned to eat what we put on the table, so has Peggy."

"They've been taught that they are lucky to have the food they have; they understand, even though they are young, that the war meant that folks did not have much of a variety in what they ate."

"My goodness," Holly gave her friend a wide-eyed look and a shake of her head.

Once the little girls had a snack, they played again in the living room.

"So swell, they certainly get along."

"Been together since they were tiny."

"Since you know me and I have no idea about anything, this is personal. Jake's been sleeping next to me since Saturday night. Today's Tuesday. Each night now he wants to touch me, and he whispers how much he loves me. I don't know about going along with him, because I don't know him yet. But I have, I guess, sexual feelings for him. I know my vagina gets wet, and he has an erection. What do I do?"

"Well, I know you two try the rhythm method, sex only during safe times."

"I don't know what that means, Cindy, explain."

Cindy went on to explain a woman's period, ovulating time, and safe times for sex.

"Would he know about, uh, do you suppose we keep a calendar?"

"I'm sure; you must do something, Holly. You're not pregnant."

She shook her head, "I don't know that; I haven't had a period since I lost my memory."

"Tonight, if you have a chance, you should approach him. I imagine he wants to have sex with you."

"I am sure he does. Why did we get married so young?"

"I guess it was what many did, celebrating the end of the war and the beginning of a new life for our country and for us."

"Was your dad gone during the war years?"

"He was; he still has nightmares about his experiences, and has a hard time talking about what happened."

"I am told that my dad got to come home early, losing his eye."

"He did; it was an awful thing to happen. But Holly, there were terrible injuries to many veterans. And so many died. Oh, our country truly suffered."

Holly watched tears come to Cindy's eyes as she shook her head. They stayed quiet together for several minutes.

"And I am so sorry that I have no memory of that, only what I am told."

"Our country is glad to be getting back to the way it was before the war; we have new hope for our future."

"What should I do about Christmas?"

"I think you might leave it up to Jake, perhaps just help with a meal for all of your family, to celebrate the holiday."

"I will check with him. Mom says he gives me money for groceries and other things I buy. But I don't know what to do for Maggie. She loves books; maybe find her a book at a store?"

"That sounds like a good idea. Holly, you are trying so hard. But you must give yourself time. It's obvious your memory isn't returning yet."

Holly burst into tears, "Oh Cindy, what if I do not get it back?"

Cindy came around the table and gave Holly a hug. She remained seated, her crying continuing.

"God's in charge, Holly, it's His Will, for you and for all of us. Please continue to pray, for yourself, and all your family. I will do whatever I can to help you. You have a part-time job at the library. If you need help with Maggie, let me know. I take care of Peggy."

"I'll call, hope to start back at the library next Tuesday, a couple of days before Christmas."

"That will be good; you will have your routine figured out by then."

"My family, and Jake's have helped me so much."

"I am so happy to hear that. We need to go, home for lunch and Peggy's nap."

"Thank you for coming over; in high school, something in my brain says, I performed in a play. Is that correct?"

"Of course, you were the female lead, Elaine, opposite Mortimer, the male lead, in the play *Arsenic and Old Lace*."

"Were you in it?"

"Yes, I was a crazy aunt, Abby."

"Next time we get together for our daughters, you must tell me the plot."

"A fun, and funny play, we had such a good time performing it; you are so talented, Holly."

"I am?"

"Yes, your folks made sure you had singing and dance lessons. You spoke about opening your own studio, to teach dance and singing, and to produce plays for the community."

"Was I starting to work on that?"

"You were. When you are feeling, like the person you will be, sorry, that sounds strange, there is a company of actors that work together, bringing community theater to Riverdawn. It's an effort since the end of the war, and you are one of those actors."

"That sounds like a wonderful opportunity; I wonder why no one has talked to me about that?"

"Your family does not want to weigh you down with too much, right now. Do you understand that, Holly?"

She nodded her head to Cindy. They rose together and hugged. Cindy took time to change Peggy's diaper and then they went on their way. Holly fixed lunch for Maggie and her. After she put Maggie down for her nap, she rested for a few minutes.

In the basement she found the clothes she hung up on hangers and put down there the day before.

"Much better, I will learn this quick, removal from the wringer and immediate hang up on a hanger, then take to basement to dry."

She took the clothes up to the guest bedroom for ironing. When she just had several clothes left to iron, she heard Maggie singing from her crib.

"I am going to get through this, I am," she teared up and then remembered to take deep breaths.

When she saw Maggie, she smiled. Her daughter smiled back from her crib. They ate together that Tuesday evening. Jake called, letting her know he would be late. She saved a plate for him. After she gave Maggie her bath and read to her, she put her to bed.

"Christmas music, yes, that will be nice."

She sat on the couch for a few minutes and read the paper. She kept seeing the words communism and Soviet Union in what she read. Jake arrived home after she showered and put on her comfortable robe.

She reheated his food and sat with him as he ate. He talked about his day at work.

"This winter weather," Holly began.

"Sweetie, I'm used to it; we just layer up, and we're just fine outside. It is actually better than the summer heat and humidity."

"Before you shower, I need to ask about sex with you. I know you want to be intimate with me. My concern is another baby. I talked to Cindy, and she says we use the rhythm method. Then she explained what exactly that was. Where is the calendar we keep, you know for the safe days to have sex?"

"I'll get it for you. Let me shower and we'll talk about it. I am happy to hear you ask about this. I always want you, Holly. You're exciting and a fun partner when we play."

They sat at the kitchen table an hour later.

"Looks like you helped me keep good records of when I ovulate." Together they looked over the calendar they kept in a drawer in their bedroom.

"Your periods are regular, and there is one coming up in several days. How about making love, say, tomorrow night?"

She gazed into his blue eyes, "You know I'm scared, Jake, I don't ever remember doing this with you."

"We'll go slow, stop whenever you say, I want the sex you have with me to be fun, loving, and an act you want to do again and again with me."

They stood together, then hugged. He bent down and kissed her, a slow deliberate kiss. She felt his tongue, probing her mouth, exciting her in her groin.

"Wow, Jake."

"Yeah, wow, I want you."

She nodded and smiled up to him, "Tomorrow night."

"Oh, I spoke with the library, Jake. They are happy with my progress and want me to return on Tuesday of next week. I need to help you, money-wise, any way I can."

He kissed her on the cheek, "And I appreciate all that you do, for me, our family, for Maggie, and for our future."

℅

"How do I look, sweet girl?"

"Petty, Mommy."

"I guess you don't see my scar or my face returning to normal color."

"My mommy," Maggie held up her arms to have her mom pick her up.

"Hug, Mommy."

All of a sudden Holly felt like dancing with Maggie in her arms. She did several dance steps and repeated them as she and Maggie flew across the living room rug.

"I declare, I am feeling more like the Holly I guess I am beginning to be."

Maggie smiled to her. Holly gave her that wide smile and set her down.

They spent the next hour and a half driving to the grocery store and shopping. Everything had a old look, the labels on the cans, Holly had to continually remind herself what year it was. She purchased the groceries based on the meals Holly learned to cook from the menus her mom gave her. On the way home Holly found a gas station. Maggie learned as soon as she could sit up straight in the car, to stay where she was. It was a strict rule, that she adhered to. Holly's head hurt as she thought about the fact that passengers just sat in a car, without any protection against an accident. She had trouble understanding why the car was that way.

Holly got out of the car and looked at the strange looking gas pump. A young man came toward her.

"I'll pump the gas for you, ma'am, just get back in your car. I'll also wash your front window.'

"Why thank you; do I pay you?"

He nodded as that sharp pain slashed through her head as she got back in the car.

"What is going on, with my brain?"

She remembered to get money out to pay him.

"That'll be $1.05."

"What, uh, how much does gas cost?"

"Right now it's 21 cents a gallon."

"21 cents a gallon?"

"That's correct, are you OK ma'am?"

"I'm not," she shook her head to him. "Please keep the change."

"Well thank you."

Holly drove away from the station, being careful of the slushy snow on the sides of the road.

"The young man deserves a little extra, for helping us, right Maggie?"

"Yes, Mommy."

After dinner that night Holly read to Maggie after she had her bath. Jake showered and joined them on the couch. He took over the reading with Maggie while Holly had her shower.

Together they put Maggie down to sleep.

"It must not happen often, the two of us doing this with our daughter."

"Agreed, it does not. I have some late nights, when I don't get to see her."

She turned to Jake after they left their daughter's bedroom. They kissed in the hall, a tongue-touching deep kiss.

They returned to the kitchen table. Jake put several items on the table while she was away showering.

Holly saw what looked like two wine glasses and two tickets. They sat down next to each other.

"I want to celebrate your returning to me, Holly, as a person who is learning to be what Holly was. Your face, it is becoming as it once was, my beautiful, beautiful one. But that blast of your wide smile, that's such a wonderful addition."

He went to the refrigerator and took out a bottle of wine. He opened it and poured wine for each of them, the first time Holly had alcohol that she could remember.

"A toast, Holly, to this Christmas time, to your return to us, a time of sharing and remembering the good life we have now, so blessed."

He brought his glass to hers and they drank a toast to each other.

"That's a nice taste, so that's what wine tastes like, any way this kind, tan-colored," Holly touched her tongue to the roof of her mouth, savoring the taste.

"And my special Christmas present to you; something you asked about months ago. I have tickets to see *It's a Wonderful Life*."

"Help me, Jake, I can't remember."

"It's James Stewart, Donna Reed, in time for this Christmas season. I read a little about the movie in the paper. We are going two nights before Christmas. We talked about it, when we read in the paper that the movie would be released in time for this holiday season. It kind of sounds like a movie celebrating a town helping its residents, pretty sure the time line is during our life time, with finishing about the end of the war. Your mom will babysit while we are gone."

"At night, like a date?"

"Yes, so Maggie will be asleep. Your mom will bring a book, and she would like to make sugar cookies, in a star shape; she'll bring the ingredients."

"That will be so nice because I don't know how to do cookies yet."

"Everything's a learning process for you."

"Yes," she looked over to him and gave him her wide smile.

"More wine?"

"Please, just a small glass, the alcohol, it has an effect," she let out a big breath.

Holly stood, putting her hand to her head.

"My head, it doesn't hurt, I must be getting better," she thought.

She felt herself being lifted up into Jake's arms. He carried her to their bedroom and set her on her feet.

"I love you, Holly."

She nodded her head up to him, but her mind said, "I do not know what that really means."

They lay together.

"My beautiful one, we have this night, to be," he paused, "to be one."

The alcohol she drank helped her as he undressed her and then himself.

She relaxed as they explored each other's bodies. Holly felt a huge ache in her vagina as he entered her. They thrust into each other, faster and deeper. Soon Holly exploded into an orgasm as Jake released his precious seed to her.

He lay on her, his penis still in her.

"My love, I missed you."

Holly thought, "Oh my, this is what a climax feels like."

He kissed her and she kissed him back. He moved from her and lay next to her.

"I hope you liked that; I know you can't remember, so this is like your first time."

"Yes."

They dozed together. Then Holly put on her pajamas and got up for the bathroom. She turned the lights off in the rest of their home. When she returned she found Jake under the covers, sound asleep. She checked on Maggie. She crawled into bed.

"Dear God," she prayed, "let me learn to enjoy my time with my husband. Somehow I know that Your Will can guide me with my future."

She gazed out the thinly-curtained window, seeing the star-lit sky. Sleep took her.

ॐ

7 p.m., Sunday, December 17, 2006, Porttown, Iowa

Evan stood on one side of Kate's bed, and her parents stood on the other side.

"It's nearly 24 hours, and she's still not coming out of it."

David and Ann gazed at Evan as he said it. They also saw tears in his eyes. He covered Kate's hand with his.

"Evan, patience, we need to pray, time, it will heal her, I feel it," Ann's voice faltered. "Tomorrow, we must go to work. I have my students, and David has court."

"And I got school, paper due, exams, the last two days before Christmas break. I'll have more time to get stuff done, since the play's over."

ॐ

6 a.m., Thursday, December 19, 1946, Riverdawn, Iowa

She put her hand next to his side of the bed, empty. She lay there for several minutes, listening for her little one.

"My ride will be here in a minute. Last night, wonderful, I love you."

He moved from the door of their room and stooped to kiss her cheek.

"Have a good day, you and Maggie."

"OK."

She heard him pull the front door closed.

"That wine, my head's exploding, like a lit firecracker."

She raised up and swung her legs out of the bed. She felt wobbly as she moved from the bedroom to the little girl singing in her crib.

"Moning, Mommy."

"Oh Abby, you are a sweetheart."

She looked closer at the little blonde girl.

"She isn't Abby, the little girl I babysit. Who is this child?"

Her head pounded and pounded, a rhythm like her heart. As quick as she could muster, she changed the diaper and rubber pants and found an outfit to put the little girl in. Her mind flashed back and forth, Abby, Maggie, Abby, Maggie.

She held the little girl in her arms and asked her, "Who are you?"

# 3

"Maggie, Mommy."

"Maggie," her mind steadied on the word as she repeated it again, "Maggie."

The little girl sat on the floor of the bedroom as her mom got into the outfit she wanted to wear for the day.

"These clothes, unbelievable, the strange styles, pants baggy at the bottoms, oh, I guess the war."

Together Maggie and her mom walked through the living room to the kitchen.

"What do you want for breakfast, Maggie?"

"Toast, mush, peaz."

She put Maggie in her high-chair. Her head blasted her heart rhythm.

"The toaster?"

Maggie pointed to the lower cabinet where the family kept the toaster.

"Oh yes, thank you, Maggie."

She fixed toast for both of them and remembered about coffee. She made a six-cup pot. It percolated on the stove. Holly heard the merry sound and inhaled the comforting smell. Then she decided.

"Mom, oh Mom, I need your help so much," she blubbered into the phone. "Could you please come over as soon as you can. Uh, is this a day you don't work?"

Ellie responded to her daughter's pleading and within 15 minutes drove to the home. She drank coffee as she watched her daughter eat the toast. They made oatmeal for both her daughter and Maggie. Ellie helped wipe Maggie's hands and face and got her down after she finished her cereal. Maggie went to her room and brought out her blocks and logs to build on the living room rug. Ellie watched her daughter, her eyes and face beginning to return to the way they were before the accident. But she cried with silent tears streaming down her face.

"What can I do to help you?"

"A memory has returned. My head hurts, but not like when I woke up this morning. My memory doesn't match all the things I've learned this past week. You may want to write some of this down. I will. And you may want to ask another person or so to listen to what I need to say."

"God is here; He is with us. Go ahead, Holly."

"I'm not Holly; my head continues to clear. And I don't believe I'm losing my mind."

"Talk to me, I'm your mom."

She shook her head to her mom. Her crying stopped, but a puzzled look continued on her face.

"Tell me who you are."

"Are you sure you're ready; I'm writing, and I want you to write, OK?"

"OK."

"My memory says I am Kate Reynels, spelled r-e-y-n-e-l-s. My dad and mom are David and Ann Reynels. I am 16 years old, and I live in Porttown, Iowa. The last thing I remember I hit my leg against a set placed behind the curtain of the stage, the Porttown High School stage. Here is where my mind is. I've my life memories, plus what I've learned the last few days as this person, Holly Schoner. I had no memory as I learned to be Holly. Now I do have both sets of memories. I am learning who Holly is. But I know now who I am."

"Sweetie," she touched her daughter's hand, "Can you tell me, do you remember the year that you had this happen to you?"

"Of course, it was Saturday night, December 16, 2006, the final night of our play, *High School Musical.* I was a lead, Gabriella. That's the last memory I had."

Kate leaned into this woman who she now knew to be her mom. "I am so frightened. Am I understanding, as I've learned, that this is December, of the year," she paused, swallowing hard, "1946?"

"Yes, it is, 1946."

"You must explain again, how did Holly get hurt?"

"Blows to her head; if you look at yourself in a mirror, you will see fading stitches and your blue eyes are recovering from the black and blue all over your face, and in the back, a cut. Let me get you a mirror."

She peeked over at her daughter playing on the living room rug and took the mirror from her mom. She looked at herself and crumpled to the floor in the living room.

"Oh, dear Lord, help me."

She got to her knees and held her hands together as she whispered out a prayer, "Help me, God, with time, my time."

She got up and went to her mom, handing her the mirror.

"I am Kate, and I have long brown hair with red highlights and brown eyes. This image, this is Holly, correct?"

Her mom nodded to her.

"So I have the body of Holly, and the mind of Kate."

"It appears so."

"Whatever we do; I'm learning about Holly, been in her body for a week."

"We go on; you and I will do your chores for Thursday, have lunch, and call Dee. I hope she can get away. And I will request that Mr. McLerner, a deacon of our church, visit with us at the same time as Dee. These are folks I trust. Will it make you feel a little better if I call you Holly?"

"I don't know; my body is Holly."

"I know you have your whole life to share with us."

"I do; am I a freak?"

Ellie got up and hugged Holly as she again cried.

Holly struggled, "It'll be a terrible idea if this information gets away from the family. A lot's happened in 60 years, to my time."

"It will stay in the family; what you are going to tell us could destroy us all."

"I don't want that to happen. Why has God done this, brought this upon me?"

"Holly, we don't know why, but what we do know is," and Ellie stopped talking.

"Share with me, Mom."

"it's what we do with what we are going to learn that is important."

"I agree; we move forward, correct?"

"Yes."

For the next several hours Holly and Ellie did the Thursday chores at the Schoner home. Ellie washed clothes, and Holly ironed the dried clothes from the day before. Together they hung the wrung out clothes on hangers in the basement. Holly swept the bare floors and cleaned the bathroom. Together they prepared shepherd's pie for dinner that evening. All Holly would have to do was heat it up; all ingredients were cooked ahead of time. They ate lunch together with Maggie and put her down for her nap.

Dee and Stan McLerner arrived, almost at the same time. The four of them sat at the kitchen table with cups of coffee, lots of coffee. Dee introduced Holly to Stan.

"Thank you for coming, all of you. My memory returns. But this you must know. My body is Holly, but my memory belongs to a teen named Kate Reynels, spelled R-e-y-n-e-l-s. Mom came over this morning; she is so supportive of me."

"I am completely supportive; I have been here through all this with my daughter, from the time she lay in the hospital, with her head injury and no memory. And for the past few days she worked very hard to relearn who she is; her blank memory is beginning to fill in with who Holly Schoner was and is. Then this morning, a mind-blinding headache came to her. And a life memory filled in.

But you must know this; it must remain between us, and you, Stan, as a witness from our church, God's witness in our behalf. Kate is a 16-year-old teen, born in 1990."

Dee and Stan shook their heads in disbelief.

"And the year she comes from is 2006. That is the memory Holly has now, the Holly from the time of her head injury, and it appears, Kate's entire life."

Dee and Stan sat, dumbfounded. They looked at Holly, this pretty young woman, who recovered from a concussion, from blows on both front and back of her head. They saw that the front of her forehead had the cut that continued to heal as her face came back to her original skin tone.

"I've heard of time travel; I know the injured mind can accomplish a great deal. Together, well we need to hear from you, Kate. May we still call you Holly?"

"Certainly Stan, from this morning I'm juggling both sets of memory, the short one from the time Holly woke up from her injury (no memory before then), and my memory backwards from when I hit my leg on a set on the Porttown High School stage to the early days of my life."

Dee designated herself as the official note taker, for the group. Holly began, explaining the Kate in her memory.

"I am a junior at Porttown High School. I have a dance and singing background, classes my folks had me take from the time I was three. As I shared with Ellie," she nodded to her, "Mom, my parents are David and Ann Reynels, R-e-y-n-e-l-s."

"What do they do?"

"Dad's a lawyer, and Mom's a middle school teacher."

"Middle school?"

Holly nodded, "that's sixth through eighth grades."

"Siblings?"

"One brother, much older, away at college, out of my life for the past few years."

"Are you aware that there is a Porttown, Iowa?" Dee asked.

"I didn't know, from my short memory as Holly. As Kate, I remember. It's a pretty community, corn country. Ethanol is an important product of our corn production; it's in our gas. My town, it's off Interstate 35 right in the middle of the state."

"Ethanol, you say a product of corn production, share why it's important?"

"Yes, one of its uses is to cut the carbon emissions of our automobiles. That's why corn is such a valuable commodity."

"Stop, Holly, these are things we know nothing about. Let's stick to personal things for now," Stan nodded to her.

"I'll share a little of my life. I love chemistry, think it's what I want to study when I go to college. So I try to use both sides of my brain, the drama, singing, dancing, and then the science side, my interest in chemistry, physics. And I'm good at science. I'm in AP Chem, uh, that's advanced chemistry. I have my driver's license, got it when I turned 16 in November. My parents got me a car to drive. I babysit a lot, for three neato kids, Sam, Annie, and Abby. Abby is 15 months old, and is a blue-eyed blonde like Maggie. When I first saw Maggie after my head injury, well, mom, you remember."

"Oh yes, you kept calling her Abby."

"Our Maggie, and the Abby I babysit, they seem so much alike, good eaters, can play alone, take naps and go to bed easily."

"That's why it's been real natural for you to take to Maggie, you have experience with children."

"Right, I started helping out when I was 12, so four years. But I want to try for a job away from kids, now that I have wheels, uh," she paused and nodded, " a car. And I plan to do summer theater, plus be in the school production in the spring."

"A boy in your life, because you certainly have one in your husband, Jake."

Holly began laughing, "Oh my goodness, last night we made love, sorry but I needed to say that. What an experience, after we'd done that, well it was the first time in my new memory as Holly. It was fun."

The three of them laughed with her. They saw a wide smile on her face, a new look for Dee and Stan, and the smile Ellie saw a couple of times since her injury.

"That smile," Ellie nodded, "that wide smile, is that Kate?"

"Yes, Kate has a wide smile, and she smiles a lot."

"So," Dee added, "your memory, sounds like, was beginning to make the transition, from Holly to Kate, early on when you got home with your head injury."

"I guess I was. Do you all like my smile?"

"Yes, of course," the three of them agreed.

"As Kate, did you have a boyfriend?"

"Evan Huan, super talented, dancer, singer, plus smart in his other classes."

"Your age?"

"Yes, he's 16; he was born in Porttown. His parents moved here from Vietnam.

"Vietnam?"

"Country in the Thailand, Korea area; America fought a war with the Communist North Vietnamese during the time 1964-1975."

"I hope we won."

"Nope, we lost that war, and several others before and since."

The three of them shook their heads, and Stan spoke out, "I never thought we could ever lose a war."

"We have."

Holly saw distinct worried looks, their foreheads lined and their tight lips.

"Let's move on, because Maggie will soon be up, and we'll need to try to meet again."

"As Mom said, what we do from here on out is what is critical. I really feel that if any of this information gets out, I'm as good as dead. Do you understand that?"

"We do, God alone knows the plan, for each of us, for our futures. You, body of Holly, and mind of Kate, you are precious to us. And what we do not understand is whether the mind of Kate will remain with what Holly knows now, or whether that memory will somehow go away."

"Remember what Dr. Abram told us, medicine is continually learning about the mind, and about memory and the loss of it. I have read a couple things about time travel, it makes interesting reading, so what I suspect is that Holly and Kate are in some kind of time travel, time warp situation. Our girl's brain, it is extremely fragile, the blow to Holly's head. And Kate does not remember what happened to her after she hit her leg against the set."

"That's correct, Ellie, but something extremely serious happened to Kate, to have her memory return in time to Holly's mind."

"Cannot be explained; and yes, I agree with Holly, if we don't keep this whole situation contained, crazy people will come after her, and all of us, for information about the future." Stan confirmed, "The future will play itself out; it's not our place to take this information anywhere but here."

"Folks, are you sure you want to know what's happened, some highlights of the past 60 years? Some of it will be very hard for you to believe."

"I think I speak for all of us. What we learn, we must take to our graves, what this 16-year-old teen's mind shares with us," Ellie nodded her head.

"What would be the best outcome for Holly, for Kate, that's what we must think about. And I believe we need to include three more people, Tom and Greg, and of course, Jake. That has to be it," Stan looked to each of them. "I have a lot of praying to do, as we sort through all this with Holly and Kate."

"I agree," Holly smiled to these folks who cared so much about her. "Perhaps tonight?"

"Yes, I can come back," Stan nodded.

"And Greg and I can come, to be with Jake, I can imagine how upset he is going to be," Dee added.

They finished the last of their coffee as they heard Maggie singing in her room.

&#8450;

The family gathered together at the kitchen table that night. Maggie fell asleep as soon as they put her down. Holly made a full pot of coffee. Stan arrived as he promised at 7:30. Jake showered after he, Holly and Maggie ate.

Ellie shared a little information with Tom, and Dee told Greg something of what she knew. The only thing Holly told Jake was that she was getting memory back.

Stan began, asking for confidentiality for everything that would be shared. Ellie gave the initial information about the insertion of Kate's memory into Holly.

"Stop."

Jake got up, paced through the living room back into their bedroom. He felt tears come to his eyes. Then he stopped in to check on Maggie.

"This feeling sorry; you have a daughter to raise; listen to them, you stupid jerk, you have to help out."

Tears dribbled down his cheeks as he rejoined the group. He asked for a refill of his coffee.

"I'm ready; we must go on."

He looked around at the faces of five people he loved. He watched them nodding their heads. Their deacon, he saw, nodded his.

"Kate is tall, like, me, Holly. She has long brown hair with auburn highlights."

Holly put her hands inches below her shoulders to show them the length of Kate's hair.

"Her eyes are brown. She loves school, the sciences, plus she's a dancer and singer. David and Ann, her parents, always had her in special classes to take advantage of her athletic ability, her dancing, singing, acting."

"Porttown High School has lots of talented students. So drama productions are a big deal. Kate got the lead, Gabriella, in the play *High School Musical*. The play came out in 2006, and her group was one of the first high school performers of the play. Her male lead was Evan, called Troy, in the play."

"Tell us about Evan."

"He'd been Kate's special friend, for about a year. Not so much a boyfriend, but a teen who had the same talents she had, the singing and dancing, and the enormous gift of science. They're both in AP Chemistry, uh advanced chem. But you need to know, groups of young people hang out together, that's maybe three or four girls, and three or so boys. Students with the same interests spend time together, not so much one-on-one dating. Evan is Vietnamese, from the country of Vietnam. His parents came to America and a little later Evan was born. They own a dry cleaning business in Porttown, and another one in a community 30 miles away. They work so hard, want the best for Evan. So from him Kate developed an important work ethic. You must work hard for what you want in the future. His parents really instilled that in him."

"He has been a great example for Kate."

Holly nodded, gave them all her wide smile, "For sure."

"That smile, that's Kate."

The group nodded their heads in agreement with Jake.

"Earlier you mentioned a war with Vietnam, a long war."

"Yes, the US got involved, lost over 50,000 solders, but the Communists still hold the country."

"The years?"

"About 1964 to 1975."

"This afternoon you mentioned wheels. Does that mean a car?"

Holly giggled, "Oh, right, Kate has a car, a 2000 Honda."

"We're not familiar with that name."

"She babysits, so needs a car to get to her children's home. Yes, Honda is the name of a popular car that Americans drive, a Japanese car."

"Japanese," Holly heard them all speak out in a loud voice.

"That's correct and another popular Japanese car is called Toyota. Many folks drive that kind of car."

She watched everyone shake their heads, "Unbelievable, absolutely unbelievable."

"The Japanese, such bitter enemies of our country," Greg slammed his hand against the side of his chair, his anger apparent to them all.

"Let's take several minutes, get up and stretch our legs. We are all going to be very upset by some of what Kate's memory, that's Holly, will tell us. That is why the information can never leave these rooms," Stan spoke in a solemn and serious tone of voice.

"Do you understand now, that what I know, through Kate's mind, it can mean my death, possibly the death of all of us."

oth her mother and her mother-in-law teared up as Holly made the last statement.

They sat back down together, getting more freshly perked coffee and eating the fruitcake Dee brought.

"There are several events I want to share. Then I think I'm pretty much done with Kate's time. She had a busy and happy life. But my memory of her ends as she hits her leg against the set."

"You have had a chance to think about the memories that hold. You decide."

"Our presidents, Truman, then Eisenhower (she heard clapping from the family), then John F. Kennedy."

"Yes, he fought in our War, in the Navy."

Holly nodded, "Then he was assassinated, and Lyndon Johnson took over."

"Assassinated, that's a terrible, terrible event for our country."

"Richard Nixon, who resigned, Gerald Ford, Jimmy Carter, Ronald Reagan."

"He's an actor we know, a president?"

"That's right."

Tthe group looked at each other, shaking their heads, with wondering eyes.

"Then George H.W. Bush, Bill Clinton, George W. Bush, he's the son of George H.W., and right now there's a Black senator from Illinois who looks like he will try for the presidency."

"Black, uh, do you mean colored?"

"Yes."

She saw wide-eyed and stunned looks on her family's faces.

"And just one more thing to share, when I was 10, on September 11, 2001, two passenger jets flew into two skyscrapers in New York City, one passenger jet flew into the Pentagon in Washington DC, and one passenger jet planned to fly into the capital building in Washington DC. The passengers on that plane tried to thwart the plane's pilot; the plane did not make it to DC, but flew into the ground in Pennsylvania."

"Unimaginable."

"That's right, that's what it was. Our country will never be the same, scarred forever."

"A war, after an invasion of our country?"

"There still is."

"Communists?"

"Can't say, but we're fighting in Iraq and Afghanistan."

"Enough, we've heard enough to have our lives come to unbelievable upheaval. Do you understand; nothing can leave these rooms. This is horrible, and completely distressing news, news," Tom paused, "that could change the course of our world."

Stan stood, "I believe we need to reflect and pray to our God, in our own way."

The rest of the group stood from the table, held hands, and let the quiet take them in. Holly heard a low and soft version of *Silent Night* coming from the radio in the living room.

Stan, Greg, and Dee left. Tom and Ellie continued to sit with Jake and Holly.

"There is so much we do not know or understand about our world, and about medicine. The human brain has so many capacities. And as doc told us, they do not know much about, honestly, about how the human body and mind work. What we must trust is that this beautiful woman, our daughter, and your wife, has had just an unbelievable experience and a terrible trauma. We all must pray and know that what is happening is God's will, for us, for Holly. I believe what has happened to Holly's brain, is one of those unexplainable things. There is no way to analyze this situation. We must love, and be loved. Do you understand what I am saying to you?"

Tom looked into the eyes of the three people sitting around the table with him.

"I believe that God gave Holly another chance at her life; she could have been killed."

"That is correct, Jake."

"Just as, Dad, that shrapnel to your eye, that certainly could have killed you."

"I got a second chance, Holly."

Ellie began, "It is time we stop; I am not certain that we should meet again. Dee gave me her notes that she took this afternoon and again, tonight. Perhaps, Holly you may want to write down a few other details of Kate's life. We must keep this information safe, secure, whatever that means, for our futures. In the meantime, we have our lives to live. And Holly, you are doing so well, adapting to your lack of memory, making a new life for Maggie, Jake, and yourself."

"Thank you for your confidence in me, Mom."

"We have each other," Tom said, "And that, after all is what matters. I had a lot of time to think about that, as I recovered from my wound. All I wanted to do was return home, to my wonderful family."

"Each day is precious, is all we've got," Ellie spoke out.

"Yes," Tom, Jake, and Holly said in unison as they rose and hugged Ellie.

Her parents left and Jake headed for bed. Holly told him she needed to spend some time, alone, to gather her thoughts.

"And I must take time to absorb all this, Holly."
"How will I go on, with all the information I have? I'll want to caution folks, about the future. But I cannot do that. I must continue to be a loving daughter, wife, and mother. That's what God's will is for me, I believe that with my whole heart. So much devastation will occur, so many world events, and all I can do is pray, cry, and keep my mouth shut.

I can look at my situation, a Holly with a week of memory, and now Kate's memory, all 16 years of her young life, 60 years from now. I must be positive, accomplish some of my goals, like my family said, give dance and singing lessons when Maggie gets a little older, participate in community theater. Next Tuesday I must welcome the opportunity to return to the library. I have a job; that is a wonderful start. And our family needs the money. I must check with Jake as to how much the hospital visit cost. And, oh my goodness, do we have health insurance? You have so much to learn, Holly, about your own past."

She took a quick shower and crawled in next to Jake. He roused for a moment and whispered in a groggy low voice, "I love you, Holly."

She kissed his cheek and answered, "And I love you, Jake."

One thing for certain, Holly knew, it was the first time she told him she loved him, in her short present memory.

ଚ୍ଚ

"It's a long day coming up for me, rest a little longer and I hope you and Maggie have a good day."

Jake kissed her on her cheek as she whispered, "Bye, Bye."

She heard the front door close and turned to her side for a few more minutes of rest. Her sleep the night before kept getting interrupted by seeing faces from the past, many she did not recognize.

She and Maggie ate breakfast together. Once the wash and ironing were completed Maggie helped her mom find her snowsuit and boots.

"We have snow to shovel, young lady, if we want to take our trip to the library this morning."

"Books, read, Mommy."

"Yes, we'll get library books for you, Maggie, and for Mommy. We'll stop by and see the folks I work with."

"Work?"

"Yes, remember, Tuesday and Thursday afternoons, your grandma comes to spend time with you while I go help out at the library."

Once she finished shoveling the driveway and sidewalks, mom and daughter built a small snowman in the front yard. Maggie put stones in for eyes, nose, and a mouth. As they took off their boots at the front door, Maggie began to cry.

"Mommy, libery," then she pointed to Holly's head, "Hurt."

Holly hugged Maggie.

"Yes, you are correct. I got hurt at the library. But I'm better, and it's OK if I go back there now. I will not be hurt."

"Sir, Mommy?"

"Yes, I am sure. You remember what happened to Mommy."

"Hurt."

Holly looked in the phone book for the library address. She had a foggy memory of the place when she drove all over town with Jake and Maggie. She felt relief when she spotted the library ahead and to the left. She did not see a parking place so drove around the block.

"I must remember to ask where I can park, for next Tuesday."

Holly felt the warmth of the library staff as they asked sincere questions about how she was getting along. She showed them the cut on her forehead and indicated the cut on the back of her head. One of the staff held Maggie, as Holly shared a little of her last week.

"I will be glad to get back." She gave them her wide smile, "I have a week of memory, and I know you all will show me again, and again," she nodded, "what I need to do. And you are wondering, yes, it looks like I have lost my memory of the past, from when I got hurt in the work room, at least for now."

She and Maggie went to the children's area and chose books. Maggie sat, looking at a book, one of five, she wanted to take home. Holly found the fiction area. She felt tears come to her.

"This is such a comfortable place, I can feel it. I have so much to learn, about everything, sometimes it just overwhelms me."

She stared at the titles and the book names.

"Pick two, Holly, maybe a book can be fun reading," she told herself. "But, knowledge exploded since this time. I know so much more than what is in these books. God help me right now; Kate wants so bad to speak out, to share, but I cannot."

She wiped tears from her eyes and mopped her nose. She found her daughter, immersed in a storybook.

"Mommy, go home, read to me." Maggie gave her mom a serious look, "I read to you."

"That sounds grand, Maggie, for you to read to me."

They each carried their books to the library checkout counter.

The assistant librarian stopped by to let Holly know that next Tuesday, Christmas Eve, the library would close at 2:30 p.m. and would not be open the day after Christmas. So Holly would only work two hours during Christmas week.

"I know you are ready to get back to work. Just enjoy your family at this holiday time, OK?"

Holly nodded to her, "OK, but I'll really be ready to come back and dig in once the holidays are over."

"Agreed, and we'll welcome you back."

Holly nodded to her. Maggie insisted on carrying two of her five books out to the car. Holly carried five books and held Maggie's hand.

They ate lunch and Maggie picked a book for her mom to read to her. She went down for her nap, and Holly hurried about, getting the wash and ironing completed while her daughter slept.

"Wow, I am proud of myself," Holly smiled and nodded her head. "Unbelievable how much energy housework takes, the laundry especially. The cooking and cleaning, they aren't so changed from now to the future time."

Jake mentioned to her about sending Christmas cards. With her new memory Holly knew he told her the cards were addressed and placed somewhere. She did a little searching and found the cards in the bottom dresser in their bedroom. And as he indicated, they were signed, had notes on some cards, and addresses got placed on the envelopes. But they did not have stamps.

"I wonder who addressed these cards?"

She decided to try writing cursive; she printed everything, from the time her mom dictated a grocery list to her. She took a written envelope to the kitchen and sat with a piece of scratch paper. She wrote the name in cursive.

"My handwriting, it's beautiful, slanted forward with nice, round letters." She was reminded of Kate's handwriting, a slanted backward sort of scrawl. Everything's word processed on the computer, gosh, cursive handwriting is almost obsolete."

Once Maggie got up from her nap they had a snack together. Then they read and Holly decided to show her what Christmas cards looked like. She and Jake picked a couple of cards, with holiday sayings.

Holly read the sayings to Maggie, and they looked at several different cards that Holly and Jake obviously had worked on before Holly got hurt.

"Mare Crismus."

"That's correct, Maggie, Merry Christmas, is what many people say at this wonderful time of year. But you also know this time as the birth of Jesus, the Christ Child."

Maggie nodded to her, "God son."

"Right," Holly thought to herself, "this little one is amazing, just like Abby's amazing."

"You are amazing, Maggie."

Maggie nodded, "Smart."

"You certainly are that."

She hugged her daughter.

୫

Jake sat with Holly and Maggie, after dinner that evening. They each read to her after her bath.

"I need to learn how to change a diaper, Holly. It's time."

They worked together to put on Maggie's diaper and rubber pants for bed time.

"How did I do?"

"You've almost got it; it's the safety pins, getting them snug."

"I need to practice more."

"OK."

Holly let Jake put Maggie down for her sleep. They said the night prayer they always spoke to Maggie.

"Thank you, God for my day. Good night, sleep tight, wake up bright in the morning light."

Now Maggie could recite the prayer with them.

They returned to the couch. Holly turned the radio volume up a notch so they could hear the Christmas music.

"I got my period today. This is another new experience. What do you remember from my talking about periods?"

"The first day, you feel crampy, and take just a bit of a pain pill, but not like the stuff the doc gave you for your head wounds."

"Oh Jake, the pads to stop the menstrual flow, they're really bad news. I can just tell you that in Kate's world women often use tampons, that insert into the vagina. They hold off the flow of blood, not near as messy as pads, which can leak."

"Advances in all aspects of medicine."

She nodded to him, "Yes, but with the head injuries, Kate had friends in sports who had concussions. The docs in that day have the same concerns as the doctor who helped me. Of course, I had an actually wound to show. Concussions are on the inside, so there have been advances, but still concerns."

"The trauma, and not knowing what to expect, the brain, quite an intricate part of the body."

They nodded to each other. Holly watched his blue eyes probing into her blue eyes.

"Is tomorrow night our date night?"

"It is; I am very excited to take you to the movie. Your mom will stay with Maggie. It is a big Christmas present, from me to us."

"I can't wait," she stopped talking, smiled to Jake, and kissed him on the cheek. "What about Sunday, what has the family decided? I remember from somewhere we share, bringing stuff, so no one has to do all the cooking."

"If you're feeling OK, and you haven't mentioned headache since Thursday morning, we will all go to church together, and then everyone will come here for the Sunday noon meal."

"What is our part of the meal?"

"Meatloaf, I know you have a recipe that you use. We'll look at ingredients, get them at the store tomorrow, and get it prepared and cooked before we go for our movie. Then all that has to happen is heating it up on Sunday, before we eat. I will help you, Holly. This is your first time having the family over. I don't want to overwhelm you."

"Thank you for that."

"Goodness, Wednesday is Christmas Day, what about then?"

"We'll forgo Christmas Eve services on Tuesday, and Mom will have Christmas dinner at noon on Christmas Day. We haven't shared this with you, but I have two older sisters, Jane and Eva. They are coming with their children and husbands. They don't live far."

"What for us to bring?"

"Nothing, we have the gift of you, returning to us, that's all they want, is Holly back. Only mom and dad will ever know about your new memories. We all understand that you have only a memory from December 12."

"Jake, you must still have huge concerns about what the five of us talked about last night."

He took her hand, "I do. I almost throw up, when I think of what you know. You gave us a taste of that, last night. And I have to let it go, just as you have to hold your tongue. I know that has to be horrible for you."

"The sadness of knowing so much overwhelms me once in a while. Then I have to clamp down on my brain, return to Holly, and take in this moment, time with Maggie, and with you."

∞

"What do I wear for a movie, like for church?"

Jake smiled to her, "Uh, usually one of these three dresses that you laid out, hose, black heels, understuff," he laughed and she joined in.

"And you have a nice dress-up winter coat, in the front closet."

They said goodnight to Maggie and Ellie and drove to the theater.

"You said the movie just came out."

"Yes, and I had the opportunity to buy advance tickets. I don't know if you remember, because you weren't home for long, but I left one evening. It was to get the tickets, our Christmas gift."

Holly loved the movie, somehow remembering several snow scenes with the banker.

"I must have seen this show sometime, as Kate, but my memory, like with some future stuff, is fuzzy."

They each shared the best parts of the movie as they sat together at the kitchen table after Ellie left. As promised she read to Maggie and put her down. They smelled the sugar cookies, carefully put away in the cookie jar. They peeked and saw the star shapes.

"My mother, she's so flexible, and cares so much."

"That goes for my mom."

"We were lucky, and blessed to have them."

"Our dads, goodness, they fought in the war that I don't have any memories of."

"They gave, some. And some," he paused, "gave all."

Holly burst into tears.

"How in the world, how in the world," she stopped and cried for several minutes, "will all these families get through the grief, the absence, of their beloved ones."

"Many will try as hard as they can."

"And some, will never recover?"

"I suspect that is correct, many broken people."

Holly got up and took their cups to the sink. Jake went ahead and got ready for bed. She sat on the couch, looking over the tree.

"Maybe next year we can think about electric lights for the tree."

Her mind whirled through the years of holiday trees Kate remembered. She said a prayer and joined Jake in bed.

ℰ

"You are doing very well, Holly, being a good hostess for us."

"It sure helped that you all brought other food. And thank you again for making the star sugar cookies. Mom, what makes the sugar cookies so soft?"

"Use lard."

"What is that?"

"I've showed you shortening, for cooking. Lard is like shortening, to give substance a moist texture."

"Like a lot of butter on a piece of toast."

"Yes, like that."

After the meal, the men rested in the living room, while the women cleaned up and did dishes. Jake put Maggie down for her nap.

Holly went to her mother-in-law, "Dee, what's wrong with these guys; they're not helping us?"

"I know."

"What would happen if I asked them to help us?"

"Don't do that."

"Why, Dee?"

"Kitchen is not men's work."

She heard a note of caution in Dee's voice. Holly's intersecting memories brought a flash of anger to her, "Don't say anything, dummy, don't start a fight, just thank goodness, in Kate's life, men do help out, in the kitchen, and with their children, they share the responsibilities of home and family."

ℰ

"Want to talk a little about Kate's world?"

"I would like to do that, Jake, we're comfortable here on the couch, and Maggie is asleep. It's Monday night, and tomorrow, Christmas Eve, I go in to the library, just for a little while. They'll close early. I'm anxious to get on with this life we have."

"As am I."

He kissed her cheek.

"I tried to go back in my memory, what I learned in American History. Have you heard of George C. Marshall?"

"Of course, he's starting to talk about countries beginning to recover from the war."

"Pictures I've seen, the devastation all over Europe."

"Both our dads have photographs from their time spent overseas."

"Are they willing to share stories and pictures?"

"Not yet, neither one of them; the memories, still too raw, and my dad, maybe never. His demons seem to be rearing their ugly heads. Thank God he had his mechanics training; he fixed up equipment, vehicles, and didn't have to shoot much, except out on patrols."

"Marshall, from 1947 to 1951 or so, through his plan, helped bring hunger, poverty, chaos, and desperation under control in Europe. People's homes, livelihoods, and futures were pretty much destroyed in many parts of Europe by the years of war; no food, no clothes, no place to live. That's been in movies, in history books, oh Jake, complete devastation for them, in body, and mind."

"That must have taken so much money."

"It did, something like $12 billion aided the European people."

"During those four years?"

"Yes, plus, there was a displaced persons plan, for somewhat over one quarter of a million. Many Europeans came to America. They got granted American citizenship."

"I've read some about that; we don't have many here yet, from Europe, but I think in bigger cities, more are coming. Many are Jewish, are coming."

"Do all Americans know what happened to the Jewish people in Europe?"

"I'm not sure."

"I want to go to bed, but I need to let you know that the bad times for the Jewish people, that's now called the Holocaust."

"You mean, the extermination of people."

"That's right; Jake, the number they always say now is that 6 million Jewish folks died in what they now call concentration camps."

"Stop, I am just glad that we are helping the folks overseas."

They checked on Maggie. Holly snuggled next to Jake.

"Early tomorrow?"

"Yes, Monday, and possibly Tuesday, early days, maybe we'll get off a little early on Tuesday, Christmas Eve."

"Each day is precious."

"Yes, and we are all on call Christmas Day, for some reason, that is often not a quiet holiday for the power company."

"Storms."

"Yes, goodnight Holly."

"'Night."

&#8449;

"Are you sure you want to?"

Mary asked Holly that, when she requested to return to the workroom where she got injured.

Mary stood with her.

"I don't remember this room. Where was the shelf that fell on me?"

She walked over to the wall and pointed to the area.

"We took the shelf away; you can see now that we have bookcases here. They are safer, not so tall."

Mary came back to Holly, "We are so sorry about the shelf. And we hope and pray you get your memory back."

Holly shook her head, "Nothing's happened, just my forward memory from the time I woke up at the hospital."

Mary nodded to her and set her to work, reshelving books. Now Holly had to relearn the whole Library of Congress books locations process.

"Whew, I have so much to learn, so slow, right now," she whispered

And soon she saw the lights flicker, letting the patrons know that the library would close in five minutes.

Holly gathered her coat and bag and waited for the other library helpers to leave. They stood around her.

"We are so happy to have you return to us."

"And I am very happy to be here, Merry Christmas to all of you."

Everyone exchanged the greeting with hugs all around.

She turned on the radio on the drive home and sang along with a holiday song she became familiar with by keeping the radio on and listening to Christmas music.

"Holly, be happy; this is the life you will be living, But you will need to continue to serve, working at the library, maybe helping at Maggie's school when she goes, doing volunteer work, and maybe helping with acting and singing," she spoke out as she pulled into the driveway.

When she arrived inside, her mom handed her the stamps she requested at the Sunday meal.

"Thank dad for me, Mom. Our Christmas cards, the few we send, will be late. How much are stamps?"

"Three cents."

Her mom watched Holly's eyes widen.

Then Holly remembered; Kate's memory just interjected itself.

"The future?"

"Mom, three cents plus 40 some cents more."

Holly watched her mom shake her head to her, and just smile.

"Maggie and I had fun, reading, and she wanted to color a picture for me to take home. Soon we will have an art gallery of Maggie's efforts in our home. There's a space on our kitchen wall, our gallery.

"Wonderful, Mom."

"Uh, tell me, I know we get mail right at our front door mail box. But I don't know what happens to outgoing mail?"

"All the mailmen, including your dad, pick up outgoing mail in the same box as incoming. Just use a clothes pin, and they will mail the outgoing for you."

"Great, that is sort of the same procedure that we have in 2006."

&#8450;

She looked up at Jake as he swung her around the dance floor in a waltz. She felt the warmth of bodies nearby. The smell of cigarette smoke coming from the tables almost choked her.

"This is wonderful; did we go to a lot of dances?"

"Every chance we got; dances were one of the few forms of entertainment during the war. We also spent a lot of time listening to the radio, for news as to how the allies were getting along."

He held her closer.

"It is so wonderful to dance with you; the new you, and I love you, Holly."

"And I love you, Jake. I'm beginning to know you, and I think we must have been friends."

"We were, best friends, and I hope we can become best friends again."

"You know the most intimate parts of me, but I am just beginning to know you. It still scares me some; you are tall and powerful."

"Have to be, to do my job."

They found their way back to the table where their parents sat.

"We love watching you dance; our Fred Astaire and his lovely dance partner," Greg smiled to the young couple as they sat down.

It took Holly a minute to remember who Fred Astaire was. She pulled that from her Kate memory, when her dance instructor talked about the early dance masters of the 20th century.

Holly kept her eyes out all evening for the demeanor of the folks at the dance. She saw many bright eyes, wide smiles to match her own, and a general feeling of good will.

"Has the VFW been doing these dances for a long time in their hall?"

Her dad answered, "They stopped, with so many men gone, until after the war. So this is only the second year of the New Year's Eve dance since?"

Greg replied, "Since 1940, the Japs invaded us, December 1941, nothing after that for some time."

The three couples stood together as they welcomed in the year 1947. After the countdown they gathered in a group hug, and each husband kissed his wife. Holly heard the sounds of horns and clapping hands.

Jake took the babysitter home and Holly checked on Maggie.

"You are our beautiful and smart daughter," Holly whispered and touched Maggie's forehead with her lips.

"Share another part of the future with me, Holly, I want to know so much more."

They sat together on the couch, with the Christmas tree and its shining tinsel in their background. They heard soft music, no longer Christmas, on the radio.

"Computers, machines called computers, come into the world in the 1950's and 60's. Calculators, to do math more easily, come about the same time. And what these new machines do is allow people to accomplish more work, like typing and math, in less time. It will make for a different world, in which to accomplish stuff. But, we can't talk about it now. The future will unfold all of this. It's going to be exciting."

"To 1947, Holly," he paused and they kissed, "may it be a wonderful year, for you, and for me."

"To you, Jake, my thanks for your patience, for trying to understand what happened to me, and for filling in parts of my past life."

"You may never get that memory back."

"I have accepted that, as God's plan for me."

"Let's go to bed, to be together, my love."

He kissed her and they finished their glasses of wine.

෩

Holly awoke at 5 a.m., her head pounding like it had 24 hours after the shelf hit her.

"Happy New Year, Holly."

"Go back to sleep, Jake. I'll take a pill for my headache, make coffee, eat something, and come back to bed. Maggie should sleep a little longer. Making love with you, glorious."

"Was terrific," he kissed her and rolled to his side.

Holly took slow steps to the bathroom and took a pill to swallow with water in the kitchen. Her head hurt worse and worse. She forced herself to make coffee and drink some. She fixed a piece of toast. After eating it and more coffee the pill started to work.

Tears spurted from Holly's eyes and her nose drained as she sat at the kitchen table. She tried and failed to pull up Kate, who rested on her mind these past days.

"God, help me, where or where is Kate?" she kept asking herself.

**2**

Tuesday, December 19, 2006, 4 a.m., Porttown, Iowa

"God, where am I?" Kate whispered.

She looked around, felt herself lying on a bed with a raised up head, watched saline solution drip into her arm. The odor of antiseptic caught her nose. She took her free hand and started at the top of her head, which pounded with a fury like large hail landing on her. Down she went to her forehead, where she felt tiny butterfly bandages.

"Instead of stitches," then she moved her head forward and felt the very sore back of her head.

"Stitches."

She moved her hand down her body, felt the tube that relieved her from going to the bathroom.

"That's gotta come out; I need to get up and get moving. What date, what time is it?"

She found the button that must be for the nurses station. She pushed the button, 1,2,3, then a second time, 1,2,3 punches. Then she waited.

Within a minute a woman in a dark green scrub outfit appeared.

"I'm awake; I want you to take out the catheter; I'm hungry and I would like to eat. And I need to get up and start walking around. I want to leave this place as soon as I can."

"Slow down, young lady. You are?"

She thought for a moment, "Kate, Kate Reynels, R-e-y-n-e-l-s.

"I'll get some help; we'll get you fixed up."

Within an hour Kate had an early breakfast, started walking out in the halls, and expected her parents.

"Can I shower, before my folks come?"

She got to do that, being careful of her forehead and the back of her head. The pain pill they gave her had an effect; she felt more like Kate.

As her pain diminished, she started remembering the dream she had while she was unconscious from the concussion. The dream stopped in her mind as her dad approached her bed.

"Oh Kate, thank you God, you gave us back our daughter."

She watched her dad drop into a chair near her bed, put his head in his hands and cry uncontrollably. She hopped out of bed and went to her dad, trying to console him. She put her arm around his shoulder. He stood up, hugged her and rocked her back and forth.

"Dad, I'm at the hospital, but nobody will tell me what day it is. How long have I been out?"

"Saturday night, December 16th."

"What day is today?"

"It's Tuesday morning, December 19th."

"I was out for about, uh," she did the calculation in her head, "56 hours?"

"That's right; we were frightened out of our minds, that you might not come out of this."

"But I did, Dad."

"Thanks, God."

"I want to go home as soon as I can. I'll go get dressed. Mom has to be at school, right?"

"Yes, she's off on break, starting Thursday."

"So I missed school?"

"Just a couple of days, Evan's kept up on your assignments."

"Dad, give me a minute. I want to tell you about what happened to me while I was out."

"Go ahead and get dressed. Then we'll talk."

She sat back on the edge of the hospital bed after she dressed.

"I dreamed I traveled back in time to 1946. I gotta talk to you, mom, Evan, and maybe a church deacon, about this."

She touched his shoulder and looked into his eyes.

"I've not lost my mind, the dream, so vivid, so real. I plan to write it all down."

"Yes, you must do that. The MRI they did on you was inconclusive; what they say is that the brain has a tremendous capacity to heal. You have a serious wound, especially to the back of your head."

"Dad, what happened?"

"A quick couple of sentences, OK? The docs have to check you out before they'll let you leave."

"Uh, what?"

"Evan thinks you must've hit your leg against a set that wasn't balanced well against a back wall. Anyway the set tipped forward, a corner of it landing on the back of your head. And you went face down, so the front of your skull slammed into the wooden floor of the stage. You have one hard head."

Kate giggled, "Haven't you always told me that, that I am so hard-headed."

"Yeah, for real, another person might not have survived that concussion," he shook his head to his daughter.

She saw his hollow, red-veined eyes.

"Thanks for bringing my clothes; I'm sure more comfortable now."

She wore blue jeans and her Porttown High drama sweatshirt. She found the brush in the bag her dad brought. Kate returned to the bathroom and brushed her hair. Finally she looked, really looked at herself in the mirror.

"Sheesh, I look like I got the crud beat out of me."

The blackened skin above, below, and around her eyes began to fade to a purplish, greenish shade. She looked closer at the red cut on her forehead.

"Wow, somebody did good with the butterflies; I may not even scar."

"Dad," she said as she returned to him, "Could you please look at the back of my head. How much hair did they have to take?"

She put her head down. Her dad separated the back hair and found the spot.

"Not bad, a small area, the stitches look clean, you have several of them, I see you were careful brushing your hair. Nurses did a good job of cleaning up the blood in the rest of your hair. You can't even see where the wound is with your top hair coming down."

"Let's go walk; they said the doc should be here in 15."

Kate looked out the hospital hall windows at the snowy scene, holding her dad's hand as she walked along.

"Christmas is coming; oh, Dad, being with the family will be my best present. Is bro coming home?"

"You bet; he's called every day to see how you're doing. And Evan's super upset. He's come to see you several times here at the hospital."

"People care."

"Totally."

"I want to surprise Evan; I'll call him when I get home, at least leave him a message."

ଛ

Kate sat at the kitchen island.

"This milk tastes so good; the milk I drank didn't taste like this, more creamy, the milk from 1946," she thought about that as she ate a chocolate chip bar.

She loved the taste of the chocolate as it melted in her mouth.

"Mom tries to make these bars for special occasions," she thought, "like when my brother comes home from school and hey maybe a homecoming for me, from the hospital."

After she asked her dad what the menu was for dinner, she decided to get the meal started. Her mom usually did that, but Kate knew, from her dream, that she cooked meals, as Holly.

They sat together for dinner; with a special grace that Kate gave, a special grace that Holly's family always spoke before the beginning of a meal.

"Sweet peace of God, watch over us, forever. Thanks for the gift of this food, Amen."

"That's an especially nice grace; I've never heard you say it before, Kate."

She signaled her dad, nodding to him.

"Kate has a lot to explain to us, a little tonight, then she's asked Evan to come over, tomorrow evening, and she would like to have a deacon from our church present."

"Punkin, what's going on?"

Kate saw the surprised arch of her mom's eyebrows.

"Believe this, or don't believe this, while I was unconscious for those several days, I traveled back in time, to 1946. My, whatever, you want to call it, got imbedded in the mind of a young woman, Holly Schoner. I will begin to write out what happened to me tonight. And I intend to find out if this woman ever existed, dad said he would help me investigate. It was such a real experience for me. Yeah, I know what you're thinkin', that my daughter's totally flipped out."

"Kate, I don't judge you," she watched her mom smile to her, "We'll take this whole experience one day at a time. We're blessed beyond measure to have you return to us."

"I'm sorry for what I must'a put you through, Mom and Dad. I've never been hurt before, not really. The docs need me to check in, once next week. And they want to make sure I'm OK, one time after that."

"We're just so glad that the sets for the play were lightweight."

"I think heavy ones would'a crushed my skull."

"That's correct; it was a good decision your drama teacher made when you all initially started on the play production."

"Porttown Community Theater is producing *Brigadoon* for late March, before spring break. I want to sign up to audition for one of the main characters in that play."

"You don't want to do a high school production?"

"Not after what happened to me; I want to take a break from that high school auditorium, from that stage, just still creeped out about all that."

"They took the stitches out before you left, the ones on the back of your head?"

"I watched them, Ann. Kate," he smiled to his daughter, "you're a tough nut. And they took off the butterfly bandages from your cut on the front of your head. It won't be long and the color will return to your face."

"Yeah, I just held my breath, as they took each stitch out."

"So you can wash your hair tonight."

"Ick, need another shower and a hair wash, after I help with the dishes."

"Punkin, you mentioned wanting to talk to us about what happened to you, during your time unconscious."

"That's right, over a period of time in late December, 1946."

She stopped talking, as her mom stared at her.

&#8449;

Kate left a message for Evan after she showered. She had no idea what his schedule was, with the Christmas break starting tomorrow. She thanked him for the instructions about her homework, and what she missed at school on Monday. He mentioned in a note he would bring her Tuesday homework by, sometime Wednesday. She suggested he wait and join the family on Wednesday evening. She had the break to catch up her school work. Kate had a great deal to share with all of them.

She joined her parents at the kitchen island after she cleaned up.

"I'm not taking anything for my head, tonight. If I have pain in the night, I'll get up and take a pain pill. I need to go off the pill. I think it messes up my thinking."

"Good idea, Kate, we've always told you to walk it off, the pain, if possible to walk it off. This is a bit different."

"Right, Mom, and I know you both have to go to work tomorrow, Mom, your last day, but Dad, I kept you from your work today."

"Absolutely fine, nothing can match making sure you're OK."

Kate put her hands to her cheeks and shook her head, "Oh gosh, my car, I saw it parked to the side of the house. How, uh, how did it get home? I know I drove it for the play Saturday night."

"Dad and I took care of it; we knew you would be concerned, and we didn't want it parked at the school overnight, Saturday night."

"Thank you for that, for everything. You two, and Evan, have been so helpful."

"We decided, Sunday morning, after church, to put the tree up."

She watched her parents stand near each other and hold hands.

"You know we've always waited for you. But this year, we felt such distress, decided that might help you awaken. And we're so glad we did, for you to have this Christmas cheer as you arrived home."

"I'm going to bed; if I get restless I'll get up and write at my desk, a story to believe, or not. But it happened to me."

She nodded to her folks, gave them her wide smile, hugged them and headed upstairs for bed.

"I have a beautiful home, and a wonderful bedroom. Folks back then, they felt lucky to have a place to live. And Holly and Jake, they had a nice home for that time, but I sure could tell it was from another era. One thing I must always remember I am blessed beyond measure to have my life, my parents, the education I'm getting. I better start being more grateful, for all I have," she whispered.

She gazed around at the pale green walls, a poster of a Christmas scene she loved hanging on one wall of her bedroom. On another wall she saw the frames with pictures of her in costume, frames for the 16 plays in which she participated since she was eight. She found her flannel jammies and put them on.

"Cloth, feels so much softer than the cloth from which clothes were made after the war."

Kate asked her folks to keep the hall night light on; something she hadn't requested for many years. And she shared that she wanted her bedroom door kept open just a little. She knew where that came from, Holly needing to hear if Maggie called out in the night.

$\wp$

"I'll try a little coffee; I'm feeling so crummy right now, didn't sleep much, did some writing," Kate spoke out to her dad as she watched him open his briefcase and locate an item he needed for his day at the office.

"Guess I didn't know you drank it. And please eat a good breakfast, maybe fix yourself an egg and some toast."

"Thanks, Dad, I'll do that."

"You'll call me if you need anything; your mom's gone in real early, in meetings until 2 p.m. Her students started their Christmas break today, but the teachers and staff have an inservice."

"I'll be OK; I'm sure I super overdid it yesterday. And I want to be ready for my talk tonight." She found the gifts she would give her mom, dad, and brother tucked under her bed. She wrapped them and put the presents under the tree.

"There it was," she pictured it in her mind, "the tree Holly and Jake had, so much tinsel, but that's the way it seemed to be back then. Holly's mom and dad, their tree looked the same way. Our tree," she stood in front of the tree, "just lots of tiny multicolored lights and ornaments. Of course, the trees that I saw, well, they had no electrical lights on them, maybe they were expensive in 1946. Anyway, the trees are different now, simpler. One thing remains over the years, the smell of the trees, for sure the evergreen smell of Christmas."

Kate cleaned bathrooms and washed the sheets on both her and her brother's beds.

"My goodness, is it ever easier to wash clothes. Today you just toss them in to wash and toss them in to dry them. Unbelievable how much work it was back then. And baby diapers, women, today, just use throwaway diapers, and no rubber pants, they were just such bad news," Kate shook her head, "whew."

After making up both beds and putting clean towels out for the whole family, Kate felt wobbly. She lay down on her bed, paper and pencil near her, for her continued writing she began in the night. After she worked on a little of what she wanted to share, she called Emma and Evan.

She nodded her head after she finished her chats with them.

"I'm sure lucky to have them as friends, thank you, God."

ℰꙮ

Evan arrived 15 minutes before the deacon. Kate met him at the door.

"Oh, Kate, you look, unbelievably wonderful. How do you feel?"

She watched his slanted brown eyes check out her face.

"Better and better."

They hugged. Kate felt Evan's shoulders heave as he began to cry.

"Oh, God, I prayed so much, I thought you might not wake up."

"Evan, Evan, I'm awake now."

They separated as he tried to catch his breath.

"My relief, it's almost making me sick."

Holly took his coat and hung it in the closet.

He held her hand as they walked through the great room to the open kitchen. He shook David's hand and hugged Ann.

"She's back; what a glorious Christmas present," Evan spoke out.

They sat together with Deacon Glascow at the head of the table and a couple on each side. A tape recorder sat in the middle of the table, ready for Kate's information.

Kate gazed at Evan. He sat up very straight and tall, more filled out than most Asian people Kate knew. Buffed, that's the word she sought.

"Thank you God, for giving me a friend like Evan," she nodded. "I hope he remains a friend, after what I'm going to share."

When the deacon arrived and before they all sat down Kate's parents took him aside and spoke in a quiet tone to him. Kate had no idea of what they spoke.

Her dad started the tape recorder.

"While I was unconscious for that time, I dreamed," she looked around at the four people watching her, "a such real dream, that I must share. Please, this can never leave this room. And Deacon Glascow is our outsider, to hear this."

"On December 12, 1946, a 19-year-old woman, Holly Schoner, S-c-h-o-n-e-r, had an accident in the workroom of the Riverdawn, Iowa, library. She pulled some too heavy books from a shelf. The shelf fell on her, sending her crashing to the floor, face down. The shelf also slashed a hole in the back of her head."

Kate stopped and put her hand first on the front of her head, the cut still visible and red, and then patted the back of her head. The group could still see the discolored skin around her eyes and forehead.

"Like mine."

She watched the deacon wince, letting out a breath that they all heard. Evan felt his eyes begin to tear up.

"Holly went by ambulance to the hospital in Riverdawn. When she woke up a few hours later, she had amnesia. With the help of her family she learned to cope, having to relearn her whole life. After Holly was home several days, she woke with me as her memory. Holly's lack of memory filled in with my life, me, Kate. She pulled her family together, her husband,

Jake, his parents Greg and Dee Schoner, and her parents, Tom and Ellie Deltan, and a church deacon, a man they all trusted.

Kate shared Holly's new memory, from when she woke up with the concussion, and then the Kate memory, of my 16-year-old life, and back, to my earlier days. Dee, Jake's mom, took notes of what I shared with them."

Kate stopped and took a sip of the decaf coffee she made for those who wanted it. Her mom put more oatmeal cookies out for all to eat.

"With my memory in her mind Holly knew unbelievable facts, that, of course, no one else knew because the facts had not happened yet. It was then that the group promised they would never share information with anyone else. Holly emphasized to them that letting out information put her at huge risk, the whole family, at huge risk. She talked about being a freak, of being killed, about hysteria, if any information got out."

No one spoke for a minute. Kate heard the purr of the heated air blowing from the floor vent.

"Time travel forward, time travel back, most don't believe in that sort of situation," David spoke out to all of them. "Kate, you went back, and Holly went forward."

"Please tell us about the family, you, as Holly."

"This is the best part; Maggie was our 15-month-old daughter, a super sweet charmer, very smart, blue-eyed blonde, like her mom and dad. Abby, the little girl I babysit for, is almost a look alike to Maggie. So a lot of what I did was take care of Maggie. And Holly's parents, they were super people, that's Ellie and Tom. But so were Jake's parents, Dee and Greg."

"And Holly's husband?"

"Jake, 19, like Holly was, they met in school, childhood sweethearts. Holly had a chance to act, be in plays, had some training in that, according to her friend, Cindy, who came to visit a couple of days after Holly got home from the hospital. *Arsenic and Old Lace*, Holly had the lead, Elaine, in that play. And we know that play, it's been around for many years, since before Holly's time in high school. So that's something that's alike in both of us, our acting. And, our injuries, to our heads, the concussions somehow opening our minds to," Kate stopped talking and shook her head, "what I experienced."

The room remained quiet as the group began to absorb what she said.

"OK, returning to Jake, so, the war raged, and both our dads served overseas. In high school Jake played sports, but in the summers he did real adult work. Back then, as in some towns still, installed power poles brought electricity and phones through the overhead lines to people's homes. Jake worked for the power company starting the summer of his sophomore year. Tall, lanky, powerful from sports, he was the perfect power-pole climber and problem fixer. Once he graduated he continued his work."

"That sounds like real tough work," Evan spoke up.

Kate watched his eyes widened as they all absorbed that information.

"Yes, it was, power outages happened; ice, snow, storms snapped power lines. He worked very long hours, one weekend a month he was on-call 24/7, and in the winter he was out in the weather nearly every weekend he was on-call."

"How did he handle all that?"

"Guys," Kate paused and smiled, "he got challenged with his work; never complained, always wore enough layers to stay warm."

"One tough man."

"Holly loved him very much. They started being intimate as juniors, and she became pregnant when they graduated from high school, in May 1945. They got married soon after graduation. Holly's injured dad came home from the war, so he got to see his daughter's wedding and the birth of Maggie. But Jake's dad, Greg, still fought in the European theater."

"What injury for Holly's dad?"

"Shrapnel took his eye; he returned to the US for rehab on his face and eyelid and an eye to replace the one he lost. He got a job right away, as soon as he was able to work, as a mailman, in Riverdawn."

"And Jake's dad?"

"Mechanic before the war, so a mechanic all throughout the war, an essential person wherever he went. He came home mute about his whole experience, but he suffered in his mind, suffered terribly, for months after he got home."

"PTSD?"

"Exactly, but it was mostly hidden by the veterans of that time."

"And the moms?" Ann asked.

"Right, both Ellie, Holly's mom, and Dee, Jake's mom, took on men's jobs in the community during the war. Ellie drove road grader to plow snow in winter, and fix roads the rest of the time. Dee drove a milk truck, delivered milk to the hospital, schools, and grocery stores. She was so strong, heaving around those metal milk cans."

"And when the war was over?"

"Ellie worked three days a week at the library, and Holly worked at the library on Tuesday and Thursday afternoons; Ellie watched Maggie then. Dee loved sewing; so a seamstress, she made men's coats and suits, in addition to women's clothes."

"What about the times, the country, all that," Evan asked, "Oh my gosh."

"Jake, such a nice man, he just took Holly as she was, with a serious brain injury. But the headaches got less severe for Holly, once she took on my memory. The Deltan and Schoner families helped Holly, they all did. None of us knew what to do with me, Kate, her memory, mind, in Holly's body. But I woke up, and so I'll never know what happened to Kate's memory."

"I'm thinking, Kate, that once some time has passed, that we can investigate Holly, because there is a Riverdawn, Iowa, and this woman might very well still be alive."

"Right, Dad, I have thought about that. She would be about 79 years old now, and yes, she could still be with us. That would be an incredible experience, to see her again."

"What I want to know is," Evan paused and looked from person to person, "now that we know the people who loved you as Holly, were helping you, can you share, like the country, and of course, what you told the family about the history you know, but that had not occurred for them."

"That was the most difficult part for me, in Holly's talks with her family, and the deacon who sat in. What could Holly tell them about the future, that would not be too distressing that they might want to talk? Jake knows the most information; we shared with each other in the evenings; it was close to Christmas.

But first, the mood of the country. While Jake and Holly were in high school, they did most ordinary school kid stuff, dances, plays, sports, but over hanging everything was the war. Every effort, by every adult I came in contact with during my time in Holly's mind, was directed to that. Men were absent; women and older children took on everything that had to be done. Every effort was for the war, to bring it to an end, to bring our men home.

Our country lost so many men. An overwhelming sadness, that's what Holly felt in her community. The radio, it was the single contact with the outside world, aside from the daily newspaper, which many folks read, cover to cover. Rationing of everything, one cup of coffee a day, very little meat to eat, people living on vegetables. The vegetables grew in their gardens, like beans and broccoli, lettuce and cabbage, potatoes and cauliflower. Folks who possibly could had those gardens. That garden effort kept a lot of folks from going hungry. Older men, those too old to serve, stepped up to take on community, state, and national efforts. Everyone worked at one or more jobs. Grief, with the anger and melancholy that went along with it, affected many families. Funerals occurred with much regularity, if not in her community, then in surrounding areas; the men coming home, one way or another.

The country's hope was peace, for our country and for our allies. In talks with Tom, Holly's dad (remember, he came home after his injury in 1944), the hope for the future, a possible end to the war, began to seem real by 1945. Then the country held its breath when VE Day occurred, and then again in September with VJ Day. And for Jake's family, his dad,

Greg, did come home, but it took him until November of '45 before he made it back to the States."

"Let's take a break for 10 minutes and start in again. Kate, I think you could talk for days about what happened."

She nodded to her mom, but said nothing.

She told herself, "That's why I'm going to write down everything I can remember."

Evan came and hugged her. They stood back from each other as he gave her eye contact.

"Where you were during those unconscious days, I believe you, Holly, that is not made-up information. And I'm sure you will share more. If I can, I would like to go with you, if you find out that there really is a Holly Schoner."

They gathered together again.

"What I can say, folks, is that the human mind is an incredible part of the body. When Holly woke up at the hospital, the doctor who took care of her shared about the workings of the human mind, that the medical profession still had so much to learn about the brain. They were beginning to research the minds of veterans who returned from the war. Back then it was called shell shock, the extreme jostling of the brain. I think we call it TBI, traumatic brain injury. Anyway the doctor did an X-ray, which was all they had to look at back then. From that X-ray, he determined that Holly's head injuries turned out to be not that serious, except for the fact that Holly lost her entire previous life history, her amnesia of people and places pretty complete. So her life memories began when she woke up those hours after her injury. That is all based on what the family shared with Holly."

"And it took you about 56 hours to wake up."

"Right, back then, and what the docs say now, the longer the person is unconscious, well, the more difficult the situation might become."

"Yes, Kate, we all prayed to God that you would wake up."

"So, not everyone felt sad after the war. There was happiness in families. And in some families where the men were gone forever, there became a peace, a sense that the loved one did all he could, and that what the family must do is go on, live a full life, in tribute, to honor the loved one who died. Some families were able to pay tribute, to honor. But in other families, there was anger, sadness, grief that did not get better. In those families, many folks wished they died with the loved one who gave their life for their country. So lives were destroyed, the wages of a war fought for freedoms that folks could not fathom. It was a very conflicted time after the war.

There was joy, but there was anguish. Christmas of 1945 became a difficult time, with so many men in transit back to our country. But Christmas of 1946, which I remember pretty vividly through Holly, it was a happier time. The country was settling, to what would be people's lives, and those affected by death of their men, some were also settling, into a lonely life, or a life of new opportunity.

Babies, the country responded to the men coming home, with such a dramatic rise in births. Our country lost so many men; it was a regeneration of people needed to help continue our country. And of course, Jake and Holly had a little girl, were pregnant before they even got married."

"How did their parents react to that?"

"Overjoyed, that a new generation was beginning. Everyone expressed happiness that Maggie was normal in every way. And, come to find out, she was a super smart little girl. For sure, Maggie was my favorite little person from that time."

Kate let out a deep breath and gave the group her wide smile.

"It's good to see her smile," her mom gazed at her daughter, "she's been way too serious through all this. Do you think it is possible that, whew, that time travel does exist?" she wondered.

"How did you decide what to tell the folks back then about the future?"

"I tried to be careful, shared about the presidents. Some names certainly surprised Holly's group."

"Ronald Reagan?"

"They certainly rolled their eyes when I shared about him."

The group laughed; it felt good to Kate that they could get a laugh out during this time she talked with them.

"What about Obama?"

"Right, I shared that a black senator from Illinois was considering running for president."

"And?"

"That shocked them, I remember either Holly's or Jake's dad called him, colored."

"Americans back then, I think, often referred to blacks as colored," David mentioned.

"And with Jake I shared about computers, space travel, the Russians launching Sputnik, which prompted the US to gear up its space program, with us landing people on the moon first, in 1969." Kate shook her head, "He found that completely unfathomable."

"Did you share with him about our underground utilities now?"

Kate nodded, "Jake, again amazed, at the equipment and the technology, coaxial cables, and utility lines underground. It helped him realize that the dangerous work he accomplished would one day be replaced. I reminded him though, that in older neighborhoods all across America, those power poles would always remain above ground. He was happy about all the positive changes."

Kate shook her head then, "But what most intrigued him, television, and phone advances, the cell phone, like now we are beginning to be able to text on our cell phones."

"Did he want to know if it made life easier for us in the 2000's?"

"Yes, of course, but with advances, well, the internet goes down, computers crash, cell phone towers crap out. Then our lives come to a somewhat complete standstill. He understood that as well.

As Holly I shared with him about the future wars. It was too close to the time that Holly and Jake's dads served in the war to discuss war with them. But Jake wanted to know lots of information about Korea, Vietnam, Kuwait, Afghanistan,

Iraq, and what would happen to those countries after the conflicts. Course we're still in Iraq and Afghanistan."

She stopped for a moment.

"And we may well be for some time to come," she heard from the deacon.

Kate looked around at the four unsmiling faces, the future unknown for her and them.

"It's time to stop; thank you all for listening. I'll continue writing about my time, but this will conclude the taping. It's exhausting for me to pull up this information."

℘

"Mom, please, I don't want to say anything to the doc about my travel back in time. Agree?"

"Yes, Kate, you and your dad want to do research on Holly. That's the next step in your journey, your travel, and let's continue to call it a dream, for folks outside our family."

"Jon, too, I don't want to say anything to him."

"Correct, your brother, something like this, we'll just keep away from his radar."

"Got it."

The neurologist chatted with Kate and her mom. He checked her over, including the cuts on her forehead and back of her head. He also asked about headaches and balance issues.

"Headaches, are better, almost not having any and not so serious; my eyes, seeing fine, and I'm practicing some of my dance steps. I'm going to try out for a community theater production for March."

"You need to return to your regular activities on a gradual basis. You're a very active person, but you'll tire more easily. It's good that you can nap a little in the afternoons. This Christmas break, well, it's perfectly timed for you. Oh, and no driving, until I see you again, in a week, understand?"

She thanked the doctor and on the way to the car with her mom she spoke out, "I plan to spend several hours every day writing out what I can remember of Riverdawn, in 1946."

ഇ

Christmas Eve, Monday, December 24, 2006

"Evan, I know you want to attend the Christmas Eve service with me at 11:30. But I'm just not feeling that well. I'm kind of weak; the doc warned me that I might have a few down days, and this is the third day I've not felt very well. Please, I'm not going to church. I'll stay home; Mom and Dad will go with Jon. The only thing I feel like doing now is resting and write a little about my dream. That's what I'm calling it now, a dream. I'll call you for Christmas, OK?"

Evan listened to her long voice mail. He teared up, "She's trying to do too much; she's sicker than she knows, and she has to take it easier," he whispered. He finished his shift at the hardware store and made his way down the street to his parents' dry-cleaning shop. He nodded his head as he entered the shop and thought, "Sheesh, the work never ends in this place."

He helped his parents finish the workload for Christmas Eve. They headed home, changed and attended the 7 p.m. mass at their church. No one wanted to stay up late that evening. Christmas Day was a rare day off for the Huan family. More than anything he wanted his parents and his sister, home from college, to relax.

On Wednesday afternoon, the day after Christmas, Evan sat with Kate. They held cups of steaming hot chocolate as they sat on the great room couch. Kate sipped her drink. Evan waited until his cooled down.

"I'm so glad you called me. Hey, your voice sounded better this morning. And I'm glad Christmas went OK."

"I think I'm a little better. This knock on my head, it's kinda wiped me out."

"Yeah, it has. So Kate, I know you have stuff you want to say. You mentioned you worked on your project through the last few days, and at night when you could not sleep."

"I have almost 25 pages of information."

Evan took a sip of his chocolate.

"Uuummm, delicious, wanta share?"

"Uh huh, I was in Holly's mind when she and Jake had intercourse."

"Whew, how was that?"

He watched her wide-eyed look as she started to speak.

"It felt kinda out of the world, Jake and Holly thrusting together. I now know what a climax feels like. Uh, you masturbate, so you know that feeling when your spew out your semen."

He put down his cup and moved his arm around Kate's shoulder.

"Yeah, like the top of my head's gonna blow off, uh, you're quite a graphic artist, that explanation, but that's how it is. Having sex, it's gotta be a super exciting time in a young person's life."

"Uh huh, not one I'm gonna experience anytime in the foreseeable future. But yes, sex is exciting."

He kissed her cheek, "Right, as you've said, it's gotta be with someone you love."

She turned into him and nodded, "Correct."

"What you want is friendship with me."

"That's it, Evan, you and me, we're so in tune with our drama, our dance, and our singing, and the way we think about, yeah, the importance of our educations. Hey, and from the way folks talked, Holly and Jake, back in that day, they were special friends, from the time they were in middle school, so they knew each other so well. Before any other part of their lives , they were friends. And they moved through the dating ritual to an intimate relationship."

"Was there any backlash from their parents, having sex, getting pregnant before they got married?"

"I don't think so; remember they were a couple for a long time, childhood sweethearts. And their dads were fighting in a war far far away. It was such a difficult and different time. Holly's best friend, Cindy, has an almost identical story to Holly's. Both married soon after high school graduation, already pregnant. And I hadn't thought about this, but if Jake had been one year older, he would've been called up, in the draft, to serve his country. So his age, it seriously saved his life, from having to go to the war. He and Holly were just 17 when they graduated."

"How did that happen?"

"If I remember right, they were super bright kids, so somewhere in elementary or middle school (they called middle school junior high back then), their teachers skipped them, I think, two grades. It didn't seem to harm them. They continued to do really good in school."

"What are your drama plans for next semester?"

"Evan, I'm not gonna do the school play; *Brigadoon* will perform in late March, the community theater effort. I want to be a part of that effort. I need to get away from the high school stage for a semester."

"That sounds like a plan; you may be pretty creeped out about what happened to you."

"Yes, I am. I gotta learn to be more careful of what's going on around me. I'm usually more observant; that move with my foot, it cost me in ways I'm just now beginning to understand."

"You mean, your travel back in time?"

"Uh huh, that, and I seriously could'a been so badly hurt. I only got one brain, and I gotta take care."

She gave him a hardened look, intent on what she just said.

"Yes, shout that from the rooftop, Kate."

They sat together in silence. He removed his arm from her shoulder.

"I gotta head for work; it'll be really slow down at the store, now that the holidays are nearly over. Lots of returns, that's what we'll deal with."

"You gonna try out for the spring play at school?'

"For sure, but I want a secondary role; it was so great having you as Gabriella. That's probably going to be the highlight of my high school drama career. I'll be finished with the play so I can run track."

"That'll be great, Evan. You are uber fast, gonna do high hurdles?"

"Yes, ma'am, they're my specialty."

"Hope I can watch you at a meet; you are so graceful, fly over the hurdles like a leaping gazelle."

Kate smiled to him, nodding.

&

"What did you think, wasn't it a wonderful production?"

Kate sat across from her parents at the kitchen island.

"You should have been Fiona."

She gave her dad a small smile, "No, Dad, I was much happier playing her younger sister, Jean."

"Yes, sweetie, the singing, acting, dancing, all of it turned out so well. I am really proud of you and of what our community theater accomplishes. You will be missed when you go off to school."

"*Brigadoon*, it was a big production; maybe one day I can direct an effort like that."

"Huge organizational skills, your director had a choreographer, sound and lighting people, costumers, I know you could do it. Maybe after you graduate college you might want to tackle something like that, given all the talents you've got now."

"Uh huh, I really don't like the lead roles, Mom, rather be in the background."

"Young lady, one day, you may find a lead role that you want. Don't give up the many dreams you have."

"To bed for me; at times I still feel sluggish. It's just gonna take a lot of time to heal, my brain, so the doc says."

"But you're doing so great."

"Thanks, Dad."

She got up and hugged her dad and then her mom.

"Thank you for always being here for me."

"Our job, but since your injury, you've really stepped up with chores around the house, and complimenting us. Your Christmas dream seemed to make you really aware, of the importance of parents."

"That's for certain," Kate nodded her head and headed up the stairs to bed.

ℰℒ

Evan spun Kate around in a fast waltz. This year the prom committee asked for a dj who could do rap as well as waltz, besides the cha-cha.

"You look so handsome tonight, your black tuxedo, makes you look slightly older."

She looked directly into his eyes; with her low heels on they were the exact same height.

"Yeah, 16 instead of 14."

"One day you will be happy to have a young face."

"Uh, maybe. But you, my beautiful flower dancer, that's how you seem to me in your lovely flowered dress."

"Thank you, Evan, this is a wonderful night for us, first prom, being together."

"It doesn't get any better than this."

She kissed him on his cheek as the song ended.

"Thank you for this so special evening," Evan whispered to Kate as they stood on her front porch.

"Yes, Evan I enjoy being with you so much," she gave him her wide smile and hugged him.

ℰℒ

The day after prom Kate's dad came to her.

"I've known for several weeks; I just wanted to make sure you had a special prom, and that your school year will end on a positive note. Your grades, you're working so diligently."

"Oh Dad," she stopped, and put her hand to her face, "Holly?" she asked.

David watched her daughter's eyes, so bright and shining chocolate brown. He nodded, "That's right."

"You've found her?"

"Yes, still in Riverdawn, possibly still living in the same home."

"Oh my gosh, and a phone number?"

"Listed as an H. Schoner in the phone book."

"Oooh, not sure what that means, but Dad, may I call her?"

"Of course, you've wanted to know about all this since you got home from the hospital before last Christmas."

Kate called Holly.

# 5

"Give me a moment, Kate, I'm speaking to a memory after a lot of years of my life."

Kate heard her teary voice.

"I am so," Holly paused, "so glad you called."

"Since my accident, since I woke up after 56 hours, I've wanted to try to find you. My dad, he's lawyer, and has the ability to locate folks."

"And, sweet Kate, it was as simple as looking in the Riverdawn phone book."

"That's right."

"Holly, if it's OK with you, I would like to drive up to Riverdawn after school is out, to meet you, to fill you in on the little bit that's happened since I was in your memory. But you have your whole life to share with me. I'm curious, excited, time travel, back to you, anyway it happened to us. I have to ask this, did you or anyone in the family ever tell any of the information that you knew?"

"We did not. But you can imagine, as all the historical times unfolded, the accuracy, it just really blew us away, Jake and I continued to meet with his folks and my folks throughout the rest of their lives, about the happenings you shared with us in my mind."

"Holly, you've lost your family?"

"Yes, Jake, as well as my parents and his."

Kate paused, "I am so sorry; and Maggie, that beautiful blonde daughter of yours?"

"Yes, still as beautiful; she lives here in Riverdawn."

"With you?"

"Oh no, with her family, she's a teacher, anxious to get out for the summer, to spend time with her husband and son and do projects."

"I have so many questions, and I want to share the 25 or so pages of information I can remember from my time, with you, in 1946."

They agreed to meet on a Thursday two weeks after school ended for Kate's junior year. Kate would make the two hour drive, come in the afternoon, have dinner, and spend the night. They would have breakfast together the next morning, continue to talk, and Maggie would drop by for an hour. Kate needed to head back down to Porttown, getting home by mid-afternoon. It would be her first road trip, by herself. After that she had a part-time job for the rest of the summer at her dad's law firm. Research on upcoming cases would be her task. Her dad wanted to introduce her to the world of law.

ℰↄ

Emma sat with Evan and Kate at the family restaurant they liked to have milkshakes at on Porttown's main street. They shared their plans for the fall.

"Something in the background, that'll be me," Kate explained.

"Girl, you've got uber, uh huh, uber talent," Emma nodded her head to Kate.

"Yeah, well, I'm looking at other things I want to do."

"I'm going to try for a lead in the fall play at school."

"You should do that, Evan. You're not doing a sport."

"Right, just running, which is my fave."

"And you're working at the dry cleaner shop."

"I have to, one of our full-timers is quitting."

"Emma, what about you?"

"Play stuff, wanta do cross country next spring. I love to run."

"So no play for you in the spring?"

"Yup, time for the sophomores and juniors with the acting bug to step up."

"Can you believe we'll be seniors?"

"Seriously, happened so fast."

They shook their heads and looked at each other.

"Seniors," they spoke in unison. Kate watched their smiles.

They each left in their own cars from the café. Kate headed for home, anxious for the next week, when she could finally meet Holly.

"I'm kinda sad I can't share anything about this with Emma. I've told Evan that there isn't anything I can share with him about Holly, except that she does exist. It'll be better that way, cannot sensationalize what happened to me, a freakish kind of gift from God."

She parked in her spot to the left of the family's two-car garage.

"Thank you God, for my life, and my continued blessings."

$$\wp$$

Friday, June 15, 2007, Riverdawn, Iowa

"Oh yes, you're the Kate, in my mind, you shared about your brown eyes and long dark hair. But it's your smile, yes, that came to me through you."

Holly met Kate on the sidewalk leading to the Schoner home.

Kate looked at Holly, adding  60 years to what she remembered.  Holly remained blonde, with the same slim build. They hugged and walked in to the home.

"Is it coming back to you, kinda the look of the home?"

"Yes, of course.  You are very beautiful, Holly," Kate nodded to her  She paused for a moment, remembering, "You rented this home, right?"

"Correct, then we bought it, expanded the back of the home, into a bigger kitchen and a sun room and enlarged the master bedroom, adding a master bath."

Kate followed her as she went to the back area.

"You can see the kitchen, the enlargement. And we finished off the basement, a big entertainment center plus a bedroom, laundry, and bathroom down there."

"Wow, your home, a lot bigger."

"We had fun, made changes, over the years."

Kate put her bag in the guest bedroom after Holly showed her the roses, her pride and joy of gardening, in the back yard. The bedroom seemed the same as in her memory, doing ironing in that room.

"Everything, so much work, back then," she whispered before she stepped back into the living room.

"Let's have a snack, then we have a lot to talk about."

Kate drank her ice tea. When Holly put out the sugar cookies, Kate took a bite and gave out a little gasp.

"Oh gosh, the cookies so soft; just as they were then, what do you do now to make them so moist?"

"Still use shortening, the old fashioned way."

"And tonight, for dinner?"

"Shepherd's pie."

"Oh wow, I remember, made ahead of time, and then just popped it in the oven for the meal."

"I'm forgetting, Kate, that these are very recent memories for you, just last Christmas time in your world of 2006."

"We'll have to stop each other, when we can't remember, or don't understand."

Kate handed her the 25 pages of word processed information she recalled from her time in 1946.

"I'll skim through this tonight, after we go to bed, thank you, Kate for this."

Kate watched Holly smile, the same wide smile Holly developed when Kate came into her mind. She kept that smile all through the years.

"Jake, you need to know, from my time here, he will ever remain the loving, constant, non-complaining, hard-working man I'll look for in a life partner. That was incredible, to be married, to have all those feelings, sexual, sharing, but most of all, family."

"Go on, Kate."

"My family, not so close, my parents with separate careers, an older brother, who involved himself in sports, school activities, scouts, church. He truly got his resume checked off to be ready for admittance at a great school."

"Where is he now?"

"A graduate program at Notre Dame, also an alum there; hey, and we are not Catholic."

Both women giggled at that.

"If he's got what it takes, that's all that matters."

"It's where he wanted to go to school. Getting back to family, oh Holly, I'll always remember the times together with your family, wrestling with what to do with the information I gave you. You accepted what my mind shared with you. I don't think your family considered you a freak, something happened to your brain, just like something happened to mine, opened up our minds to unexplained situations."

"Kate, you know the answer."

"The answer?"

"To what was going on; my family accepted me for what I was, Holly, badly hurt in her brain from an accident. Love, they loved me. Remember how I struggled, once you came to me, I seemed to do better. I had a memory from when I woke up with my head wounds plus your memory back from 2006."

"Love is the answer."

"Yes, plain and simple, God loves us, asks us to love one another. That's what we did Kate, and I know when you got home from the hospital and started to share, that your folks loved you, and I imagine were extremely grateful that you weren't more badly hurt."

"Right, they talked about how blessed we all are, me healing, and us being able to have Christmas. But, it did take me a while to start feeling better. I did too much the first day or so that I got home from the hospital. I was weak for quite a time. It distressed me, a 16-year-old teen feeling like a much older person."

"But you did start feeling better?"

"I did, and I shared that on one of the last pages you'll read. But I want to hear about your life, please start with Jake, from that morning I left your mind, January 1st, 1947."

"I tried, I tried, so hard," Holly stopped as the tears came to her, "give me a minute."

She gazed at Kate and squeezed her hand that rested on the table. She took a deep breath and exhaled.

"There."

Kate nodded encouragement to her.

"I sat at the kitchen table, having coffee and toast, early before Maggie and Jake woke. I could not pull you up in my mind. It scared me so bad, the headache really bad, but I went through that first day of the new year. I accepted that the only memory I had was from when I woke up in the hospital, after the accident. And to this day, I remember nothing about my life before my accident.

When Jake woke, I told him what was going on. Once again, he accepted me, giving me comfort, helping me through the bumps of a lost memory. His patience, was incredible, with me, all through the years. And Maggie, as she grew from a child to a teen, she stood by me. We shared about my lost memory, the amnesia, when she got older. But we did not share about the future history that we already knew. It was hard at times for Jake, and me, and of course, her grandparents, to keep our mouths shut as events happened.

The accuracy, of what my brain knew, from you Kate, it seemed to be somewhat of a dream, as stuff kept unfolding. That's when we began to understand that some kind of time warp, something, had occurred to the two of us, and to actually find out that you exist, from your phone call."

"Well, I know it truly blew me away when my dad shared that there was a Holly Schoner who lived in Riverdawn, Iowa."

"I am so glad you are here, to Jake, what a wonderful husband and lover, and father to Maggie."

"What happened, he worked a difficult and dangerous job with the power company?"

"Yes, he continued as a climber for ten more years. By that time, the later 50's new equipment got developed to allow machines to hoist the employee up to fix whatever issue was presenting itself. That meant a little less danger. But still there were the downed lines, and difficulties with trees in the lines.

He continued to work for the power company, and as the years went on computers, as you told us, Kate, helped the personnel manage power grids. In 1992 he retired; his firm, called an energy company, by that time. We planned a cruise, for a month after he retired. His first weekend home, his first retirement weekend, he didn't wake up on Sunday morning. I had let him sleep. I found him on his side, the same peaceful look I saw from him when he first woke up, all our years together."

Kate shook her head.

"Natural causes, that's what the autopsy decided."

"Whew, that's for sure the way I would like to die, Holly."

"Me, too."

"And you?"

"I took that cruise, by myself. And I had a good time, 'cause, even though no one else could see him, Jake was there with me, the entire time."

"I can believe that, Holly, based on all the things that have happened. Did he eventually go away?"

"Yes, my memory of him, began to fade, a few days after I returned from the cruise."

"Still talk to him?"

"Yes, every night, after my prayers; he's always in my heart."

"And you, Holly, what happened after that?"

"I continued to work at the library. Oh, you can't know this piece."

Kate nodded her head up and down, three times.

"OK, I worked my way up, and became the head librarian. I took classes at the then new Riverdawn Community College.

I got an AA with the kind of classes that would help me with a library, business, humanities, a little computer."

Kate patted Holly's arm, "That's so totally awesome; you were some older?"

"Yes, about the same age as other students' parents."

"So you worked, and went to school, and as I see here, you really helped with your home. What about children, other kids besides Maggie?"

"When Maggie was three, that's not long after you were with me, I got an infection. There would be no more children. And Jake and I were content, one wonderful child was enough."

"You were able to give her that education you talked a little about."

"We were; she had a scholarship to the U. of Iowa. And we helped her with her undergraduate degree. She did a masters on her own, financially."

"You mentioned she's a teacher."

"Yes, at the secondary level; she also took some counseling classes, so she teaches three classes, and counsels students the rest of her day. She's married to a fellow teacher in the district, different school, and we have a grandson, Tom, 11."

"Named for your dad."

"Yes, your parents and Jake's, good lives for them?"

Holly nodded, "They had, yes, good lives. After what those men faced, in the war, unfathomable to the rest of us."

"Break?"

"Yes, let's, it's pretty toasty out back, but let's go there. It's just absolutely incredible to have you here with me."

"Thanks, Holly, I feel the same way."

After the break they sat under a maple tree. Kate heard the whispering of the leaves above them.

"Maggie asked to come over to meet you tomorrow morning, before you have to leave. It's incredible to learn that you do exist. For certain I want to remain in communication with you."

"You have internet, e-mail?"

"Yes, I do; it rattled Jake's mind as I talked to him about the coming age of computers. With you in my mind, I tried to share with him as much as I could, that I thought was important for the future. And look what's happened, Kate."

Holly smiled to Kate.

"How much of the future did you share with Maggie?"

"Not much, it kept getting harder and harder as she got older, to keep the future from her. But, that agreement that we made with our deacon and parents during the final days of 1946, we kept to the agreement."

"Otherwise, you all would."

Holly stopped her, touching Kate's shoulder, "We'd a never made it out alive; a total disruption of our world."

They sipped their tangy lemonade. Kate plunged ahead.

"Did you ever decide to share you acting, dance, and singing talents with young people in Riverdawn?"

"My goodness, you remember me being in the play, Elaine."

"So?"

"Yes, when Maggie was ages 6 to 11 I had a dance studio, worked with students on Saturdays and during the week on Wednesdays. It was my day off at the library. It was the way I wanted to serve my community; culture, entertainment for our town. My students went on to perform in dramas, school and church productions. Several did drama and singing at the collegiate level. "

"You opened up young people's minds to the many possibilities out there."

"Yes, there was and still is tremendous talent in our little community."

Kate gazed at her, "And in my town, also, Porttown has Community Theater, which you'll read about in my pages. Truly there is talent, in almost every person, if you can just bring it to the surface."

"And the most special part, one of my students from the dance studio, she returned to Riverdawn after college and pursuing a career away from here, well, she returned. As an older adult, she's opened a dance studio, including the modern stuff, and yoga."

"History keeps repeating itself."

"It does, and it makes me proud, that someone else sees the talent, possibilities, opportunities out there. And now it's for adults, and some older adults."

"Taking yoga?"

"I did; it was fun, and it helped me move on from Jake."

They found their way back into the cool home.

"I'll let you rest a bit, Holly. I want to take a walk, to see if I can remember where the library is, and the main street."

Kate walked at a brisk pace and found herself in front of the newly renovated library. She could not pull the old look of the library in her mind. But then she saw the sign set near the entrance. It had an artist's rendering of the old library, and how it transformed to the new facility using just the same space.

"I'll need to ask Holly if she was part of the renovation, the early days of thinking about the change."

Kate headed back to the Schoner home. She gazed up at the lovely trees. Then she stopped, dead still.

"Oh my gosh, they still use the power poles in this part of Riverdawn."

She looked, up and down Holly's street. Mixed in with the big trees were power poles, still bringing electricity and communication lines into people's homes.

"That's not gonna change; generations of Jake's will still need to work on the overhead lines."

After dinner that night, Kate called her parents. She spoke of how pleased she was to meet Holly, of how glad she was that she went to the place where her mind had taken her when she was unconscious.

Both she and Holly turned in early. It was hard for Kate to fall asleep, the memories of her time in Riverdawn flashing like the frames of an old time slide projector, in her mind. She finally opened the blind, looked out at the star-lit sky and fell asleep.

⅋

"Coffee?"

"Oh, yes please, Holly, I must have started liking it while I was with you. It tasted so good."

Kate ate a big breakfast of bacon, eggs, toast, and hash browns.

"You remind me of Maggie, she was such a good eater."

"I remember oatmeal, she ate that."

"And as years passed, she ate breakfast with us, with her dad when she could, but I always fixed good stuff."

"Breakfast, the most important meal of the day."

"That's right, Kate. And thank you for your writings you brought me of what happened to you before and when you left my mind. I always and forever wondered. And now I know; you were a part of me, those hours you were unconscious; now I've filled in a lot of information. As you may ask, the information we wrote down, my family and me, from the two sessions I had, well, Jake and I shredded that information, eventually."

"As I figured you would, to keep yourselves safe; it still remains in your memory, Holly."

"That's right."

And because you let me meet you and spend time with you, I have the 60 years of happenings in your world, from the time my mind left you."

⅋

"Hi Mom."

They hugged.

"Maggie, this is Kate."

Kate and Maggie gazed at each other. Kate pulled up a picture of the little girl she got so well acquainted with when Kate came into Holly's mind.

They shook hands.

"You are just a grown-up version of the Maggie I got to know, as beautiful as I expected you would become."

Maggie nodded to Kate, "And you, Kate, Mom described you quite perfectly, to dad and me."

Kate smiled to Holly, who smiled back to her.

"And there's the smiles, like Mom always told me, your wide smile, Kate, and Mom's smile, one and the same. The story goes that Mom had a quiet and somber look about her, that is until you invaded her mind, Kate, for those days in 1946 when you were in my mom's mind."

"It took me a while, when I woke up from being unconscious, at Christmas time last year, to understand what happened to me. I sat down with my family, and a deacon from our church and shared."

"Yes, just as mom said she shared with her family and a deacon, at that Christmas time of 1946. And she told me how your dad found her, your dad, a lawyer, with detective skills."

"It's incredible, Maggie, a phone book was the answer, the Riverdawn phonebook. Your mom, in that book, all through her life."

"For you two, an incredible story, which I'm assuming will be basically between the two of you."

"Yes, Maggie," her mom gazed at her, "It will remain forever that way."

"Time, past, present, future, all parts of our world, God's world, for us."

"Just accept, and go on."

"It's what my special friend, Evan, has mentioned to me many times since Christmas."

"A very smart, and special friend."

The women nodded and smiled to each other.

Maggie said her goodbyes, and Kate followed soon after.

"We will continue to communicate, Holly, I'll write, and e-mail. We're a part of each other."

Holly walked Kate to her car.

"Maggie will e-mail you and me with the pictures she took of us this morning."

"Thank you, Holly for everything yesterday and today."

Kate began to cry, which prompted Holly to cry. They held on to each other.

"A somewhat glorious gift God gave us, Kate, to be part of each other's lives," she whispered to her.

"Yes, a glorious gift from God."

They stepped away from each other. Kate put her bag in the back seat, got in and started her car. She waved to Holly and watched as Holly waved back.

Kate drove through town, looking left and right at the main street, smacks of pictures in her mind of the 1946 street, pummeled her. As she headed out, she had to find a place to pull over for a minute.

"I didn't tell her I love her. I'll have to let her know, let her know," Kate nodded, as she pulled back onto the highway, headed for Porttown.

&⊃

"Incredible, it was an incredible experience to meet Holly."

That's all she shared with her parents. But when she got the pictures from Maggie's e-mail she printed them off. She showed her parents again, Holly, Maggie, and her, in pictures, together, and separate. Maggie also sent her a picture of Holly's home.

Kate took time with her folks as they sat together. She explained how the house looked in 1946, and what Holly and Jake changed in their home.

"I'll never forget putting clothes through the washer ringer to get the water out of the clothes. The washer was a Bendix, I remember that, a reconditioned one. Nothing got built during the war years, except what was needed for the war effort. They put the laundry room in the basement in one of the renovations of the home.

You cannot believe how hard doing the wash was back in those days. And the diapers, no such thing as disposable diapers."

"Ironing?"

"Yeah, every day, it had to be done to keep up; and fabrics were harsh, not soft, like our cottons today. Mom and Dad, life was really hard back then, even the simple things."

Kate teared up as she shook her head to her parents.

"And then the men, who suffered so much during the war. They are the greatest generation, to me, that's for sure."

Her dad gazed at her, "Lesson learned from what you went through in Holly's mind?"

"Yes," she looked from her dad to her mom and nodded, "a very sincere appreciation for all that I have today, of all you have given me, your time, your energy; I can never repay you for all of that."

They stood and Ann came around to hug her daughter.

"Our job, to take care of you, Kate, and we do understand your appreciation. You gave us quite a scare, your accident."

"Uh huh, I was surprised at how long it took me to get stronger."

℘

"Can you meet me at the track?"

"When, Evan?"

"How about 7:30 p.m.; it's important, Kate."

When she got to the track behind the high school, she began to run, before long catching up to Evan, as he slowed down.

"Geesh, thanks for waiting until now, it was so hot and sticky, earlier today, the breeze's cooled stuff down."

"Let's pull over here, Kate, and sit down."

They sat down next to each other and hugged. Evan drank from the water bottle he carried with him around the track.

"Mama's broken her leg in two places."

"Oh Evan, you've lost an employee at the shop. What are you going to do, this makes two?"

"Go to work full time at the shop."

"Your mom?"

"Surgery tomorrow; the doc's gotta put a pin in two different places."

"So difficult fractures."

"Right, she fell from a stepladder, getting supplies from a shelf, lost her balance."

Kate instantly thought of Holly, on a step ladder in the Riverdawn library work room.

A plan formed in Kate's mind.

"How can I serve?" the question pounded in her head.

"If I were you, some thoughts for you," she looked directly into his dark eyes, " I'd contact Porttown Community College (cc). You have so many credits, I bet you could take the study class for the GED in the afternoon, and get it, by before Christmas. It's almost August. I will help you, Evan, I can help you and I want to. I'll come in at 2:30, after my last class, man the register, work on the books, relieve you so you can go out to school for your class. Your papa won't need to hire anyone else. We can make this work; you'll have your GED, I'll have helped you, and your shop can go on.

Then spring semester, you can work full-time, ease your mama back in as soon as her leg heals up. She's got to have physical therapy. You can apply for school; they take folks with GED's especially with your outstanding background in science and math, your AP courses. And you may want to start out at the cc, get some of your basic classes, cheaper, before you head to a four-year school."

"Oh Kate, all that you just mentioned, it sounds doable. My stupid ego will take a whack, I wanted to graduate from high school, with one last drama production under my belt."

"Your family, Evan, I found out through my recent experience, is what matters. Not sure what matters most, but anyway, it's what we're all doing, trying to take care of each other. If we don't have our families, what," she paused, dropped her eyes from him, and swallowed hard, "what do we have?"

"Families care, any way we need to have people care for us."

"Evan, your mom and dad work so hard."

"Right, they feel so blessed and happy to be naturalized American citizens, to own their own business, to have a home. What they hear from the family, what's left of it in Vietnam, is pretty heartbreaking."

"So, take what I've mentioned, those suggestions, see what your folks say."

"I will; I cannot believe it. I felt so sick to my stomach when I got here and started running. Just to get the adrenalin going, it lifted my spirits, and I knew when you got here, well, that."

He stopped talking, dropped his head and cried out, "God help us."

He began crying and Kate put her arm around his shoulder and held him.

"Evan, oh my gosh, does your family have medical insurance?"

"Yes, we do have; we didn't for a few years, but as my sister and I grew they realized it was critical. But insurance will not cover everything for mama. We'll take a big hit. I hate to say it, my mama's wages, yes, she got paid. Papa wants her to have social security, he pays himself too. With not having her salary, it will be hard."

"If I come to work for you, I just want minimum wage. I must do this to help out, my gift, from me to your family."

They drank their water, and Kate got up, giving Evan a hand to pull him to his feet.

They held hands as they headed for their cars, parked next to each other, in the lot.

"I've got another week helping dad with research at his office. Then I can dig in to learn the work at your shop."

"And I'll contact the cc. Thank you, Kate, for thinking on your feet about all this."

"I picked up a lot of abilities, when I was unconscious, about how to do stuff I had no idea how to handle."

They hugged, separated and started to get into their cars.

"You had some kind of education, during your time."

Kate put her finger to her lips, "Back to now."

He nodded.

℘

Halloween 2007 approached in Porttown. The corn harvest finished, and farmers and townspeople alike breathed a little easier. Evan and Kate sensed a change in the air, in the financial air of the area. The car industry, the banking industry, and several others, mortgage companies, in the whole country seemed to be in trouble. They heard comments from the customers at the dry cleaners. And they saw a slight decline in the numbers of items folks brought in to be cleaned.

"Hey Evan, my app in at the U. of Iowa. I should hear before too long."

She stopped in back, getting the laundry for a customer. Evan stood nearby, working on one of the machines.

"I'm glad for you, Kate. Mama's making very good progress, getting stronger each day. She's anxious to get back, but the docs say it'll be Christmas, before she's cleared from her physical therapy."

"I'll have my last semester, but I'm a little sad it won't be with you."

"OK, I really think I'll be ready for the GED before Thanksgiving. And maybe I can do what you suggested, take a class or two in the spring, get those basics out of the way before heading out, still want chemistry."

"Found the outfit, gotta head up front. Everything's progressing good."

She gave him her wide smile.

"Agree."

She grabbed the dry-cleaning and headed to the waiting customer.

જી

"Where's Evan?"

"Still at work, Pete; he hasn't seen a single football game this fall. Thanks, guys, for saving me a spot in the stands. So glad I layered up; snow later?"

"Yeah, there's a chance. This is the only game you'll see, Kate."

"I had other stuff going on, helping Evan, that was critical for me."

They cheered and laughed and almost cried during the third quarter of the football game. And Porttown lost, by one point. It was the end of games at home, the last two, out of town. All three of them felt a little down, like they had colds coming on, so they went their separate ways, rather than gathering with other friends after the game.

Kate kept up her e-mail correspondence with Holly. She shared with her how she felt so done with high school, especially after what happened with the time travel she experienced nearly a year ago.

Holly e-mailed back that she hoped Kate would try for one last drama event in her high school career, coming in the spring.

"Sweet girl, you certainly changed directions, for this fall, taking as many business classes as you could, and thinking that accounting might be a solid major for you in college. Like I did, you could one day teach dance or singing, something that you love. And you know how impressed I am that you are helping out Evan, and his family business. Families have life-altering events, as we both are aware of!"

At Thanksgiving Kate wrote, wishing Holly and her family a peaceful Thanksgiving.

"You're not going to believe this, but, Holly, the drama teacher made a decision. We're doing *Arsenic and Old Lace*. It'll be the school's spring effort, in March before spring break. I'm definitely auditioning for Elaine's part. I guess time isn't a factor in plays that have appeal year and year."

Holly let Kate know how she hoped she would get the part, as Holly had, back those years ago.

∽

Kate stood at the kitchen island. Her dad stopped near her.

"The past several weeks, Kate, I can tell, the shop, helping Evan, is getting harder and harder for you. You have lots of homework some nights. Are you getting enough sleep?"

"Some nights, no Dad, but Christmas is coming, so I know I can hang on. Finals will be over at the same time that Evan's mom comes back to work at the shop. I don't know what I'll do with all my time."

"You'll relax, enjoy being home, listening to music, practicing your dance and singing, which you've had to stop doing."

"Yeah, Dad, I'll get back into it. I haven't shared with either you or mom, but a favorite play of mine will be performed in the spring, the school drama presentation."

"And you'll try out, right?"

She watched his lined forehead, arched eyebrows.

"Uh huh," she gave him her wide smile, "I plan to audition for the lead. I sure know I can do it. But I have to finish my commitment to Evan."

"I'm so proud of you, stepping up to help a special friend."

"Thanks, Dad, and thanks for starting all the meals during the week, when Mom doesn't get home. Next semester, I'll take back over most of the cooking, so we can eat earlier, and I can get on my homework earlier."

Kate made it through her finals and worked her final afternoon at the shop.

As she was getting ready to leave, Dan Huan came to her. He touched her shoulder and smiled.

"We could never have done this, without you stepping in, for Evan to get to the community college to get his GED. He's out of high school now. And we know you suggested to him that he go on and start his basic college classes next semester, our thanks to you, Kate."

"Helping your family, that gave me much joy, and now peace, since your wife will return and Evan's come so far this fall."

"Joy and peace, yes, it's almost Christmas, I hear that in what you're saying."

They hugged each other. Evan watched from the back, tears burning his eyes. He already said his goodbye.

"She's an unbelievably sincere friend, and I will always love her. But she's got to go on. Our paths are separating," he whispered as he wiped his tears away.

ℒ

Christmas Eve morning Kate headed for the track at school. When she could that fall she ran. It helped her get her thinking straight.

"If I get Elaine, it'll be non-stop play until spring break. And after break, it'll just be a push to graduation. You think you might know what you want, Kate, but things can change in an instant. It's been over a year now. And I'm changed, forever, by what happened, what traveling back in time did, what it taught me."

She cruised around the track, following a bigger runner a ways behind her. He continued to run, faster and faster and soon caught her.

"Hey."

"Hey."

"Seen you out here before; you cross country?"

"Nah, drama, but I love to run, steadies me."

"I've watched you in the production of *Brigadoon.* I really liked you in that play."

"Yeah?" she asked, giving him a smile.

"Uh huh, I enjoy community theater, also. You have a lot of talent, Kate. Uh, we haven't ever been formally introduced, I'm Chris."

They continued to run side by side. She heard his labored breathing, in and out, spewing a cloud of vapor as he continued.

"You had a very fine football season."

"Yeah, thanks, but that life is over. I'm going away to school, hoping Northern Iowa, and if I can, based on grades and taking the MCAT; I want to study to be a doctor. What about you?"

He turned and gazed at her.

"Should hear from the U. of Iowa before long."

"Know what you're gonna study?"

"Accounting, it'll supplement my love of music, dancing, singing, being in productions after college."

Chris laughed, "Sheesh, you are really planning ahead."

"Yup, gotta have a masters in order to sit for the CPA exam. So I have five years ahead of me, but you?"

She stopped talking and slowed down.

"Yeah, eight years, then internship, residency, then a specialty."

"A lot ahead of you, but sounds like you have a plan."

"I do."

"I'm gonna go round one more time; Merry Christmas to you and your family."

He nodded, "To you, and yours."

She picked up her pace, listening to her feet moving along, and to her heart, the pump, pumping going along. Chris moved along, to the right and a little behind her. She hardly heard him, so light on his feet, and not a sound of breathlessness now, compared to the heavier breathing earlier.

Kate slowed as she came around the final curve of the track. She stopped and bent over a little to catch her breath. She now felt the cold, like a  freezing fog swirling around her.

"I'd like to go out with you, Kate, may I call you?"

"OK," she grinned up to him.

"Take care."

"Take care," she gave him just a partial smile, her full smile reserved for Evan and her family.

        And Chris did call her.  They watched a movie together at the renovated downtown theater on Porttown's main street. After, she treated them to a large brownie, ice cream, whipped cream, chocolate syrup, pop, and two spoons.  It took them awhile to eat their way through the dessert.  They shared about the people they dated, Evan, and a girl basketball player Chris dated for a while now.

"I have to move on, from Evan. He's already taking classes at the cc; got his GED before Christmas.  He's a college guy now."

"And Casey, she's a junior, and I want her to date other guys. "

"That's the same for me; Evan wants me to see other guys."

"It's hard."

"Yeah, I got comfortable with Evan."

"Like I did with Casey."

He walked her to her front door and she thanked him for the movie. He patted his tummy and thanked her for the yummy dessert.

"I'm tied up for the next eight weeks with the play. Maybe we can do something, after that."

"If that's what you want, Kate, I'd like to see you before then."

"Don't want to lead you on, but it won't happen. Sorry to be so blunt, but I have the female lead, and it's most likely the last time I'll perform on stage for quite a long time. I got admitted to the U. of I. And it'll be accounting for me, I've decided."

"I haven't heard back yet, but I applied to Northern Iowa and one other."

They hugged; Kate unlocked the door and let herself in. She couldn't shake the uncomfortableness she felt being with Chris.

"He's very self-assured, kinda creepy, I wonder what he sees in me?" she asked herself.

Chris got into his car and drove away from the Reynels home.

"She's beautiful, an accomplished performer, but around me, she seems meek and a little unfriendly. I need to examine how I come across to people. I know some of it has to do with my size."

He stood 6'3" and weighed 210 pounds. And he vowed he would ask his folks about how they viewed their own son.

ℰℭ

"You were fantabulous, Kate."

"Think so?"

She watched Evan nod his head and smile that smile of his that she just loved. They sat across from each other at their favorite café downtown. She heard a purr of noise and friendly chatter around her.

"Your dancing, the way your voice carried all across the auditorium, and the way you handled Mortimer. The play is so funny, in spite of the arsenic aspect of it. Emma, she got extra rounds of applause, for her rousing portrayal of one of the crazy aunts."

He held her hand as she watched his shoulders heave.

"I'm trying not to cry, but I love you, Kate."

"And I love you, Evan."

She squeezed his hand.

"We both gotta go on. We're in such different worlds now. You, the shop and school, me just figuring out graduation, the summer, and then off to Iowa City."

"All the time you helped us, last fall, never a word of complaint, how did you do that?"

He watched her chocolate brown eyes sparkle into his.

"The Christmas dream, the concussion, I learned what it meant to help others, our soldiers, serving our country, fighting for you and me; because it was the right thing to do, helping their buddies, to the left and to the right of them, on those battle fields. Sorry, that dream, that time in the past, will never leave me. I wanted to help you, plain and simple, it's what friends do; they help friends."

∞

Kate went out with Chris twice since the play concluded. On the third date he asked her to dinner at a favorite Italian restaurant in Porttown. They talked about graduation and beyond.

"I'm volunteering at Memorial. It'll be one way to see if the medical scene is anything I'd like to do."

"What'cha do?"

"Kitchen, getting dinners to all the patients. It's a tricky maze, delivering the separate meals to so many different patients, some with special dietary situations. It takes quite a bit of time."

"So each patient picks his own meal from a menu?"

"That's correct, and then we have to deliver the meal to the patient's room in the time frame based on when the patient made the phone call to dietary."

"You've got a regular restaurant, in a hospital."

"That's the philosophy of Memorial."

"So you have to have some tall hustle."

"Yeah, a little like running on the football field, time's always of the essence."

"Whew, how many days a week do you help out?"

"Mondays and Friday afternoons, the days when the dietary staff are down a person or two."

"Taking time off?"

"Yeah, that, and not showing up for work."

He gave Kate a disgusted look, shaking his head.

"They don't get paid very well."

"That's right, kinda minimum wage. Uh, what're your summer plans?"

"Help dad with research; mom and I will spend a long weekend with her parents in Fayetteville. They have a commitment during the time when I graduate here. And they want to see me before I head off."

"Yours?"

"Assist in running youth sports camps for an outfit that does that through the summer, all through this part of Iowa. Ready to go?"

"I am, the meal, delicious, and thank you Chris."

"Want to walk in the park?"

"Yeah, let's."

They walked along on the concrete path through the first part of the well-lit park.

"Come to the prom with me."

She turned to him and smiled her wide smile, the first time he saw it.

"I thank you for the invitation, but this year, there are four of us, friends, who want to go as a group, Emma, Pete, Sam, and me, to our final prom."

"Sheesh, I had my heart set on dancing with you all evening, you're so graceful and I'm sure light in my arms."

She heard his tone, especially his words "had my heart set on dancing." Kate heard anger in the tone of his voice.

"Chris, I know you are very used to getting your own way, about everything in your life."

"I certainly am."

Kate knew it then. She crossed the line, and he was mad.

"Time to head back to the car for me."

"Hey," he grabbed her arm, "I want a nice kiss, for the dinner, for the time we spent together."

She tried to shake his arm off her. With his brute strength he lowered his lips to hers and kissed her hard.

"I didn't want that kiss or any advance from you. I am walking home."

He started to bend his head, trying to kiss her again. She aimed for his Adam's apple with her elbow. She hit him as hard as she could. The blow dropped him to his knees as he struggled to breathe.

She shouted, "No advance from you, I am walking home."

Kate knew a shortcut to her home, through a wooded area. She made her way along as quick as she could in her low heels. She kept looking back. He did not follow her.

Her parents were in bed when she got home. Kate went straight to her room, silent tears streaming down her face. She shook so hard she had to wrap her arms around herself and sit on the floor next to her bed. She calmed down after a few minutes of deep breathing.

She shook her head with one last thought about Chris.

"That guy, no way he's doctor material."

❦

She told her mom the next morning, before church.

"I'll stay away from him, Mom. He's a big guy, but he's gotta learn respect for women. He can't treat me, or any woman like that. I didn't owe him anything, except the thank you I gave him."

"Good, stay away from him, be with friends, and well, maybe no dates for a while. I'll tell your dad, and just remember there are toxic people out there, this one toxic for you."

"I'll try to make smart decisions, like not going for a night walk on a date. Oh, Mom, my life's gonna change so fast, in the next couple of months. I still want to see Evan."

"He's so special to you." Her mom hugged her and whispered, "And I know you love each other."

"We do, but we love each other enough to let each other go. I know he wants something in drama, but like me, he'll have to have a major and a profession where he can make money."

"So he can do his hobby."

"Just like you, accounting so you can one day dance and sing."

"Got it."

ം

"I'm happy. Are you guys happy?"

She saw nods and smiles from Pete, Sam, and Emma.

"This is for sure a nice way to enjoy a prom, to be together with you guys," Sam nodded.

Kate's folks picked Emma and her up after the prom and dropped Emma at her home.

"Go home?"

"Yes, please Dad and Mom, last year was so special with Evan. And this year, I felt happiness to end the dance seeing you folks watching us from the sidelines."

"It was fun to watch you; you are just a fabulous dancer, Kate. Who was the white-haired gentlemen you danced with, your last dance."

"Just so awesome, he was Grandpa Joe, Sam's grandpa. The story goes that Grandpa Joe did not have a prom in high school, not sure the circumstances. So Sam invited him to ours. He didn't sit with us, but he did dance with Emma and me. It was a long ago wish come true."

"That's so nice, Kate. Good for Sam to invite him," she heard her dad say as he turned to her.

ဆာ

"We wanted you to have this, a sort of graduation present from us. It's actually a portfolio of all the efforts you made throughout the years. One of the interns at dad's work created it from the videos we carefully preserved."

She watched the video with her folks, surprised at how much she improved over the years, in her acting, dancing, and singing skills. Her parents clapped and clapped as they remembered scenes they had not watched for many years. And for graduation she felt happiest that Holly would be able to drive down to the ceremony and stay overnight at Kate's. She wanted to return the favor of Holly meeting her the summer before. Her dad's parents would not be able to drive in for the ceremony. Kate invited Evan, now a college student at the local cc.

The family gathered at a restaurant outside Porttown to celebrate Kate's graduation. She asked not to have a party, that she just wanted her family close. Evan sat on one side of Kate, and Holly sat on the other side of her at the circle table in a corner of the large restaurant. It ended up being the quietest area. Folks chatted and celebrated Kate and her accomplishment.

"This is only the beginning, folks, I've got the bachelors and the masters to go for."

Holly answered lots of questions about the World War II years and after that. The group, of course, was aware of what happened to Kate and Holly. But Kate wanted to call their relationship her Christmas dream.

Her parents retired early that evening, giving Holly and Kate time to talk together.

"I'm so happy for you, Kate, and you know what makes this so special?"

"What's that, Holly?" Kate smiled to her as they sat at the dining room table drinking decaf coffee and having pieces of the chocolate cake Holly brought as her graduation present to Kate.

"When you were with me, you knew I'd lost my memory of everything before I got hit by the shelf, that amnesia."

"That's right."

"So I have no memory of graduating from high school."

"Wow, so, was this your?"

Holly nodded to Kate, "Exactly, this was the high school graduation ceremony I could not remember.  Through you, seeing you walk across that stage, my dear, I graduated.  It's a grand feeling, really, even more special than when I finished up my classes at the Riverdawn Community College."

"I'm so glad that's what you got from my ceremony.  That's so totally awesome."

They chatted for a little longer and then retired to their rooms for the night.

⁊つ

"For my special friends, I wanted to do this breakfast for you.  Holly, you have to get back, and Evan, I know you'll head to work.  I asked your dad, special, and he said it was OK, to eat hearty"

Kate served up a pile of bacon, lots of hash browns, scrambled eggs, and English muffins, warm and oozing with butter.

"Feast of a king, Kate, thank you," Evan nodded to Kate.  "Oh, and yes, feast for a queen, Holly.  It's so wonderful to meet the actual Holly from Kate's Christmas dream."

They ate and ate, with Kate refilling coffee and orange juice.

"I know we both have to get going, Kate, but I want to share something with you.  You'll remember *Brigadoon.*

"I most assuredly do, played Fiona's younger sister."

"You two, I saw it, the Riverdawn theater group did it several years ago, so I'm familiar with the story."

"Remember Mr. Lundie, the village school teacher?"

Both Kate and Holly nodded their heads to Evan.

"Tommy can't get Fiona out of his mind, really loves her."

Holly added, "So he returns to Scotland, the magic of Brigadoon reappears."

"And Kate, what Mr. Lundie says in the story is what I feel for you, maybe someday. Anyway he says that if you love someone deeply enough, anything is possible, even miracles."

Tears spurted from Kate's eyes.

"Oh, Evan, I love you, are you my someday miracle?"

"I don't know, but we have a witness here," he paused and gave Holly a studied look.

They all laughed together.

"Walk me out, please Kate."

She walked him to his car parked in front of her home. The smell of the neighborhood lilacs tickled their noses

"Thank you for breakfast; it was good to spend time with you and with Holly. I am so glad she is a part of your life now. Your grandparents are far away, so she's a grand addition."

"I love you, Evan, always and forever, close in my heart."

"And I love you."

He kissed her on her forehead and they hugged, a long hug of remembrance.

He waved and she waved back as he drove away. The tears stood large in her eyes.

She returned to the table as Holly finished her coffee. Holly looked into Kate's eyes.

"You, you've been mightily blessed to have that young man in your life."

"I have been, and to have you, Holly, in my dream and for real."

℘

"It's Chris."

"Uh, hello," Kate replied in a quiet voice.

"I'm a jerk, Kate. And I am so sorry for how I treated you at the end of our last date. Please, could we meet at the little café on main, just for a half hour, maybe after you get off work, next Thursday. My sports camp is in town."

Holly thought about it for a few seconds, and decided that it was a public place, the café, and it was daytime, so she agreed.

She arrived first, and he appeared two minutes later. They each ordered a milkshake, chocolate for Kate and vanilla for Chris. They agreed to pay for their own treats.

"After what happened to us, I did check in with my folks about how they saw me behaving with people. They were super blunt. And they think you did exactly the right thing, letting me have it, for my actions."

She gave him a piercing look and raised an eyebrow, "Chris, I do not like to get physical with anyone. But with you, I had no choice. You need to know that once I had a chance to think about it, I decided that you were sure as hell not doctor material."

They each took a sip of their milkshakes as she remained quiet.

He gazed at her and paused. Then he nodded, "That's exactly what my folks said, being very blunt and honest about it."

"What now?" She gave him direct eye contact.

He nodded to her, seeing the glow in her brown eyes.

"Respect, appreciation for others, walk a mile in the other guy's shoes, those are things I must learn."

"That's for sure, otherwise, you're not going to have very many people to care about you."

"It helped a lot to do the hospital volunteer work. "

"The school for you?"

"Admitted to Northern Iowa, biological science, I got hold of a recent MCAT study guide, it'll be a very busy four years. I can do it, that's for sure. Still thinking accounting for you?"

"Yes, a profession to feed my drama desire."

He watched her wide smile and nod.

80

After she graduated, Kate worked lots of hours at her dad's firm. The summer sped along, the 4th of July with her friends, and before she knew it, the time came for her to leave for Iowa City. She decided to leave her car back home. Her parents agreed.

"Maybe after freshman year, I'll be ready to have it. But I like the idea of walking and getting around under my own power," she shared with her folks. "I like the snow, so walking in it to classes, it'll be OK. I'll need the exercise."

Kate's parents drove her to school.

"I'll admit, Mom and Dad, I'm scared and excited," she said as they arrived at her dorm.

"But I gotta do this, like getting up on the stage and singing and dancing." They helped her carry in her essentials for her dorm room. She had one last container to bring in. Her parents agreed with her when she asked them to go, that this last load into her room need to be on her own.

She stood in front of them at the SUV. They hugged, and all three of them cried.

She let go, stepped back from them, and tried to smile. She wiped away her tears.

"Thank you for my life, for taking care of me, and loving me. I love you, Mom and Dad. I am missing you, already."

She picked up the container and turned around to walk away. But she turned back to them. Kate smiled her widest smile and gave them one nod. She saw their tears. She turned toward the dorm, where students, parents and helpers scurried about.

Kate carried that last plastic container of her possessions. She noticed many bright faces of students like her, also carrying stuff into their dorm rooms. She became unsteady on her feet as she walked up the ramp.

"Here, let me help you, my task for the day, helping move students in."

A tall slender young man with blue eyes and blonde hair stood in front of her. As she handed the heavy container to him, a rivet of cold shock hit her, a shock of recognition.

"Jake, oh my gosh, Jake!"

He smiled the smile she remembered.

"Hey, how do you know me, uh," he paused, "my name; I'm not wearing a nametag?"

She nodded to him and gave him her wide smile.

# OLD CROOKED ROAD

Hope and her dad, Skip, lovingly sing and play guitars together. They carry on without Hope's mom. Hope assumes the housekeeping and cooking chores when she is 10. Beginning at 16 she works summers as a nurse's aide at her community hospital. She remains a quiet and serious student, outstanding in calculus. Hope makes a decision her senior year to study nursing in order to obtain a nurse practitioner (NP) designation.

She and Shane date during the summer, drink lots of booze and explore their sexual relationship. Hope becomes pregnant. Shane accepts his responsibility and asks Hope to marry him. Hope divorces him after she miscarries their baby. She moves forward through pre-nursing and nursing school. She joins Alcoholics Anonymous at the insistence of a friend. Now sober, she completes her NP and moves to San Francisco in 1978. Hope's mother, Faith, finds her at the hospital where Faith volunteers and Hope works.

Hope falls in love with Mark, a fellow alcoholic, and an RN. She runs a nonprofit medical clinic in downtown San

Francisco. With her NP training she writes prescriptions, performs minor surgeries, and advocates for her patients' rights. Hope continues to see more and more young men dying of an unexplained auto immune deficiency. A challenging opportunity comes for her to take over the nonprofit clinic of a dying doctor in north Georgia.

She brings changes to the clinic to improve patient services. Hope saves Joel's leg. He asks her out after his leg heals. They explore their pasts. He is a widowed Green Beret. Their love for each other grows. Joel's viniculture project expands, and many more patients visit Hope's clinic. They marry. Jared is born to this happy family. Hope finds serenity, embracing the preciousness of life.

# About Cathleen

## WWW.CATHLEENELLIS.COM

Cathleen Ellis is a Colorado native. She and her husband, John, live in the northern part of the state. They have four sons, three daughters-in-law, and four grandchildren. Cathleen draws the inspiration for her love stories from the lives of young people with whom she has lived and worked her entire life.

www.ingramcontent.com/pod-product-compliance
Lightning Source LLC
Chambersburg PA
CBHW050413110726
47899CB00008B/2693